Defense of Sinanju

The assassin stood in the shadow of the trees behind the practice putting green of the country club.

It would be easy, he thought, as he watched the mercenary colonel march up and down in front of the entrance to the building, carrying his submachine gun, carefully checking to his left, to his right, behind him, over and over again, a narrow military man carrying out a narrow military operation.

The assassin had been told there were two new bodyguards, an old Oriental and a young American. They were probably inside the house. Just as well; he would deal with them later. First things first.

The assassin moved out of the shadows, cleared his throat, then slowly slipped behind a tree.

The colonel looked up at the noise and saw a figure moving behind a tree. He went into a combat crouch and began moving across the putting green toward the spot he had seen the movement. . . .

The assassin looked across the twelve feet separating them. He pulled a silver-bladed knife from the back of his belt and raised it over his head. His hand flashed down. This time, there was no calculated near-miss. The knife burrowed into the back of the soldier, cutting through his clothes, flesh, muscles, and severing his spinal cord. The colonel dropped without uttering a sound. His machine gun made a faint little *thwop* when it hit the night-dampened grass of the forest floor.

Now the assassin only had to deal with Remo and Chuin. But he didn't know that. Too bad.

The Destroyer

POWER PLAY #36

by Richard Sapir & Warren Murphy

PINNACLE BOOKS   LOS ANGELES

DESTROYER #36: POWER PLAY

Copyright © 1979 by Richard Sapir and Warren Murphy

All rights reserved, including the right to reproduce this book or portions thereof in any form.

An original Pinnacle Books edition, published for the first time anywhere.

First printing, March 1979

ISBN: 0-523-40158-2

Cover illustration by Hector Garrido

Printed in the United States of America

PINNACLE BOOKS, INC.
2029 Century Park East
Los Angeles, California 90067

Don't Read This Dedication

This is another improper dedication, which one could expect from improper people. In all these books, not one properly colored person has been honored by a dedication. There are many whites. The pages are littered with whites, but that is not surprising considering that the cheap white help who write these books tend to favor their own ilk. There are blacks. Many of the books are dedicated to blacks but not one properly colored person has been honored.

Why We Don't Care

It does not matter that I, Chiun, Master of Sinanju, who have made Sapir and Murphy rich beyond their wildest imaginings, have never been honored. Nor has any other properly colored person been honored, not even a Japanese or Thai, let alone a Korean or anyone from north of the 38th Parallel. I do not mind. Having dealt with Sapir and Murphy, I am well accustomed to basic ingratitude. I don't want a dedication.

A Simple Demand

What I do want is to review all future dedications, lest anti-Koreanism, virulent anti-Koreanism, slip its ugly tentacles into these very pages that should honor the House of Sinanju, on the beautiful West Korea Bay, possibly described as cold and bleak and rocky by those infected with anti-Koreanism.

Pskowski Not Korean

The first four names submitted to me are Pskowski, Cumerford, Freeman, and Cook. The last two are clear. A slave was given his freedom and therefore called Freeman. His name is David Freeman. The second obviously works in a kitchen and her name is Tammy Cook. (I have a vast knowledge of the white mind and its naming systems.)

Cumerford? Pskowski?

Yet in no English-Korean dictionary will you find a Cumerford. Or a Pskowski. And without verification, I cannot allow their dedications. One can be a Shoemaker or a Baker or a Tailor but nowhere have I ever seen in a book of vocations a Pskowski or a Cumerford.

Therefore rejected for dedication are Marge and Walter Pskowski, Mary and Jim Cumerford.

Saved Whose Life?

The Pskowski dedication came with a note that Walter Pskowski had helped bring Sapir to a nearby hospital, possibly saving Sapir's life in some way. And this brings up one of the problems of America. Many of you have suffered from junk mail, useless information which wastes your time reading it. That note about the hospital was junk information. There are few things less important in this world than whether Sapir's life is saved or not, and I have neither time nor inclination to ferret them out. I think the truffle season in the Loir Valley might be less important than Sapir's life.

Then again, there are people who like truffles. As far as I know, only Murphy likes Sapir.

> In my awesome magnificence,
> I am, with moderate tolerance for you,
> Chiun, Master of Sinanju.

Power Play

CHAPTER ONE

His dark, pin-striped suits were hand-tailored in London and cost over eight hundred dollars each. His shirts were single-needle white-on-whites that were custom-made for him for ninety-seven dollars and his shoes were black soft Italian leather slip-ons that cost two hundred eighty-four dollars a pair at a small bootmaker's in Milan. Wesley Pruiss bought twelve pairs at a time.

And he still looked like somebody you'd expect to see in the back seat of a bus bound for Baltimore.

Nature had not been kind to Wesley Pruiss. She had not given him the face or physique of a leader of men or a captain of industry. Instead, he was medium height with a medium weight problem. His hands were small and soft and his face was fleshy without being fat, the kind of face that had no discernible bone in it.

But Wesley Pruiss was a man with an idea. Before him, there had been three major revolutions in men's magazines. First, there was nudity, then pubic hair, then total tastelessness. Pruiss was the fourth revolution.

"If you like your magazine dirty, you'll love it when it's *Gross,*" had read his first national advertisement. His first centerfold had been a photograph of an exquisite dark-haired woman, made up to look as if she were only fifteen years old, sitting naked on the back of a giant brahma bull that was sexually aroused.

The bull issue was snapped off the newsstands of America within three hours. His second issue was devoted to horses, all kinds of horses, bays and roans and palominos and Arabians, all stallions, all in heat. It was in the second issue that Pruiss made his next great contribution to the American sex magazine. He moved his main photo spread out of the centerfold and put it on the inside back cover with an extra fold-out panel. This got rid of the staples in the model's belly and made the picture more suitable for framing.

He also started to develop the distinctive Wesley Pruiss photographic style, which meant having his female model in very soft focus, as if seen through a fog, while the animal in the picture was stark and sharply outlined.

He was asked how he did it and replied that a lot of people rub vaseline on their lenses to get soft focus pictures.

"But how do *you* do it?"

"Me?" he said. "I rub my lenses with KY jelly because there isn't anything vaseline can do that KY jelly can't do better." The same issue had featured a long, scholarly article on sheep tupping and why it would always be more fulfilling than making love to cows and horses and goats and chickens.

At first, the press had tried to treat Pruiss as an

aberration that would go away, if ignored. But they found it impossible. *Gross* was selling two million copies a month and had to be dealt with as a full-blown national phenomenon. It didn't hurt either that Pruiss always travelled in public with a retinue of beautiful women and was not reluctant to share them with whatever reporter came to interview him.

He knew he had it made when *Time* magazine did a cover story on him. The cover was a full-color cartoon of Pruiss, surrounded by beautiful women and by horses, bulls, sheep and goats, and its headline was:

"Wesley Pruiss. King of the Beasts."

Pruiss expanded into the nightclub field. Inside three years, he had opened eighteen Gross-Outs, nightclubs in big cities across the country, staffed by Grossie-Girls who worked topless in rooms that served liquor and topless and bottomless in rooms that didn't. A feature of each Gross-Out was a Plexiglass cage suspended from the ceiling over the main bar. In it, women dwarfs go-go danced naked.

The drinks were called Sheep Dip and Horse Dong and Bull Shot and sold for four dollars each, and the gift shop in each club did a brisk business in items like monogramed personal vibrators and molds to make your own frozen mayonaisse dildo. They also sold a lot of C-batteries.

The very first Gross-Out had been opened in Chicago and after a month of operation was picketed by women's groups who thought it was demeaning that grown women should be called Grossie Girls.

Pruiss replied to the press that none of the Grossie Girls were grown women. "I only use jail bait in my clubs," he said.

The women's groups were not pacified. They pick-

3

eted the club, claiming that Pruiss was unfair to women. This was a viewpoint not shared by the Grossie Girls themselves who, counting tips, were averaging seven hundred dollars a week and paying tax on only three hundred dollars. They were not about to give that up for the honor of being called "Mizz," so they called the protest leaders to a consciousness-raising session, beat them up and stole their clothes. The lawsuits were still pending.

In fact, lawsuits were pending everywhere. It seemed every time Wesley Pruiss turned around somebody else was suing him or filing charges against him; he kept a staff of twenty lawyers working full time on salary just to defend him. And every time a new lawsuit was filed, and the press reported on it, the sales of *Gross* magazine went up and the night-club business expanded. And Pruiss got richer and richer and the magazine, the cornerstone of his empire, got wilder and wilder.

He now used pictures sent in by readers, in a department called "Readers' Slot." "Send us a picture of your slot in action," read the promo piece. The winning photo each month won five thousand dollars. Last month's winner was a woman whose specialty, if widely adopted, would have eliminated the world's flush toilet industry.

He had another standing feature called "Easy Pieces," which featured pictures of women, taken unawares, as they walked along the street. The pictures were accompanied with text that made long, lascivious guesses about the women's sexual habits and preferences. There were seven lawsuits pending on these unauthorized photos too.

Wesley Pruiss once figured out that if he lost every lawsuit and had to pay all the money demanded in

4

the court complaints, he would be out 112 million dollars. And it didn't bother him at all. All he needed was ten minutes headstart and he would be on a private jet for Argentina where he had stashed enough money to live like a pharaoh—or a publisher—for the rest of his life.

So it wasn't lawsuits that occupied Wesley Pruiss's mind on a fresh spring day as he sat in his office on the seventeenth floor of a triangular building on New York City's Fifth Avenue.

First, where was he going to find a place to film the first picture of his new film division, *Animal Instincts*. He had applied to New York City for permission to film inside city limits. The application had asked for a brief description of the film. Pruiss had written: "The story of a man and woman who find happiness in nature—she with the collie and he with her, a goat, three girlfriends and Flamma, a girl who belly-dances while Sterno flames from her navel."

The city's letter of rejection had just arrived on his desk.

His second problem of the day was to find a model to pose for the main layout in his August issue. The layout was supposed to show a girl making love to a live Mako shark. He had never realized how frightened women were of sharks.

The third problem was those goddamn women marching downstairs in front of his building. Even through the double Thermo-pane windows he could hear them.

He got up from behind his desk and opened the sliding windows that looked down over Fifth Avenue. As he did, the chants of the women below grew louder.

From seventeen floors up, the women looked small,

5

the way he liked women to look. Small and down around his feet. There were twenty of them carrying placards and signs and marching back and forth, chanting "Pruiss must go" and "*Gross* is gross."

Pruiss's face reddened. He grabbed a portable bullhorn he kept on a table next to the window, clicked it on, and leaned far out the window.

"*Gross* is gross," came the voices.

"Gross, hah?" Pruiss shouted. His electronically magnified voice swelled over the street and the women stopped chanting and looked up.

"I'll tell you gross," he yelled. "Three hundred and fifty million a year. That's gross."

One of the women also had a bullhorn. She was a former congresswoman who had been causing Pruiss trouble since he started the magazine. He had offered a ten thousand dollar-bounty in *Gross* for anyone who could write about an unnatural sex act he had performed with the woman. There were no answers. He raised the reward to twenty thousand. Still no takers. He broadened the category to include natural sex acts. He still got no replies. After running the advertisement in *Gross* for six month, he finally dropped it and did a cover story on the woman, calling her "America's last virgin. And why not?"

The woman aimed her bullhorn at him and shouted "You're sick, Pruiss. Sick. And so's your magazine."

"Never been healthier," Pruiss shouted back. "Three million readers a month."

"You belong in an asylum," the woman yelled.

"And you belong in a zoo," Pruiss shouted back. "You want a job?"

"Never," the woman called.

"I'll hire all of you. For photo spreads."

"Never."

6

"I'm booked up on girls for the next three years," Pruiss yelled. "But I got openings for two cows, a jackass and a lot of pigs. You all qualify."

"The law will get you, Pruiss," the woman bellowed back. The other women around her began chanting again. "Pruiss must go. *Gross* is gross."

"What do you have against making it with a bull?" Pruiss demanded. "You ever make it with a horse? Don't knock it if you ain't tried it."

Passersby had stopped to listen to the electronic debate, the participants separated by almost two hundred feet of open space.

"Hey, you. You with the flowered hat," Pruiss called. "Don't tell me you ain't made it with a bull."

The woman with the flowered hat resolutely turned her back on Pruiss.

"If you ain't made it with a bull, you ain't made it with nobody," Pruiss shouted. " 'Cause who else would stick it to a cow?"

"You're sick, Pruiss," the woman on the loudspeaker called.

"Go away, you dykes," Pruiss yelled. "The slut of the month feature is booked up until 1980. I'll call you then."

He closed the window, put down his bullhorn and with a sadistic smile went to the telephone.

"Send a photographer downstairs to shoot pictures of those dykes," he snarled. "If they want to know what for, tell 'em we're starting a new feature, 'Pig of the Month.' "

Pruiss was inspecting the page proofs for the next issue when a woman walked into his office. She was dark-eyed with long black hair that trailed straight and full down her back. She wore a thin white dress of some jersey material that clung to her full body as

7

she moved. She had three file folders in her arms and she smiled at Pruiss as he looked up at her.

"What do you want first? The good news or the bad news?" she asked.

"The good news."

"There is no good news," she said.

"Still having trouble with that shark layout?" Pruiss asked.

The woman nodded, and some of her hair splashed forward onto her shoulder. "Still tough," she agreed. "Everybody's afraid they're going to get their boobies bitten off. We can always use Flamma to pose for it."

Pruiss shook his head. "Flamma's done too many gatefolds already. I don't want to make it look like we can't find girls willing to get screwed by a shark."

"I'll do it then," the woman said.

"Theodosia," Pruiss said. "You know how I feel about that. You did the first one with the bull. And that was enough. Those dingdongs that buy *Gross* will have to get off on somebody else. Not you, you're mine."

"Aren't you sweet?" Theodosia said. "I'll keep interviewing. We'll get somebody."

"I know," Pruiss said. "What about the movie?"

"We just got turned down by New Jersey."

"Why the hell'd they do that?" Pruiss asked.

"They said they didn't like the content."

"Did you tell them I was a Jersey boy myself?"

"I did even better than that," Theodosia said. "They set up this commission to bring movies to the state so I had lunch with somebody near that commission."

"And?"

"And I offered him five thousand dollars. And Flamma for three months."

"And he still turned you down?"

Theodosia nodded.

"Jerks," Pruiss said. "Don't they know I'm the wave of the future? A hundred years from now, people will look back and call this the Pruiss era."

"I told him that. He seemed more interested in the five thousand dollars," Theodosia said.

"But he turned us down anyway."

"Right."

"Maybe we should just go ahead and shoot the damn thing," Pruiss said. "Shoot it anywhere."

"They'll kill us," Theodosia said. "Even if you do it on the estate, they'll kill us. Some blue nose'll get in and see what we're doing and before you know it, all our asses . . ."

"Don't swear, Theo. It's not ladylike."

"Sorry. All of us will be before a grand jury and then in jail."

Pruiss nodded glumly, then in a small burst of anger, pounded his tiny fists on his desk.

Theodosia walked behind him and began massagin his neck muscles.

"There might be a way," she said.

"What's that?"

"There's a county for sale in Indiana."

"A county?"

"Right. A whole county. It used to have one industry, something to do with knitting. Then that folded. The whole county government went broke and now it's for sale."

"What's that got to do with *Animal Instincts*?" Pruiss asked.

"Buy the county and it'll be yours. You can do anything you want there."

"I'll still get busted," Pruiss said. He tilted his head

9

to one side, so Theodosia could work on a particularly irritating mass of tightness in his neck.

"How'll you get busted? Every cop and every judge will work for you."

"The people will go apeshit," Pruiss said.

"Cut their taxes. That'll quiet them down," Theodosia advised.

"It won't work," Pruiss said. He sat upright in the chair and flung his hands into the air. "Unless . . ."

Theodosia worked around the clock for sixty hours, putting all the details in order. And one day later, Wesley Pruiss bought Furlong County, Indiana. With a check. From his personal account.

He was the owner of 257 square miles of American heartland, mineral rights, water rights, fields, town hall, police departments, county courthouse, everything.

He announced it to the world at a hastily called press conference in the New York Gross-Out club. For the occasion, the Grossie Girls were almost clad and the dwarf-a-go-go had been closed down.

"Why are you buying a county?" one of the reporters asked. "What do you want with a county?"

"Because there weren't any countries for sale," Pruiss said. When the laughter had subsided, he looked earnestly at the reporter. "Seriously," he said. "For a number of years, I've been concerned with the nation's energy crisis. The government seems unwilling to break the stranglehold the big oil companies and the Arabs have on America."

"What's that got to do with you buying a county?"

"I'm buying Furlong County to make it a national laboratory for solar energy," Pruiss said. "I'm going to prove that solar energy can work. That it can heat

10

and light and cool and power an entire American county. And to that end, I'm putting all the resources of *Gross* into the project. We're going to make it work."

He looked around triumphantly. Staff members applauded. Grossie Girls sitting in the audience next to the press members nudged them into applause too. Pruiss looked around the room, nodding vigorously, then stepped back from the microphone and whispered to Theodosia:

"Yeah, we'll make it work. But it may take twenty years. In the meantime, we'll make our movies too. Tell me, did you check? Do I own the sun in Furlong County?"

"Honey, you *are* the sun in Furlong County," Theodosia said with a tight-lipped smile.

The people of Furlong County had been prepared to be outraged when they heard that Wesley Pruiss, that filthy disgusting easterner with the dirty filthy mind who thought money can buy anything, had bought their county. Then they received letters from Pruiss announcing that whatever they had paid in real estate taxes last year would be cut in half this year. They decided they could not understand what all the fuss was about. After all, Mister Pruiss had a right to make a living and nobody forced anybody to read his magazine, and if you didn't like it, you didn't have to read it, and that, Mister Gentleman from the New York Times, is what freedom of speech is all about, and we're surprised at you all picking at a fine gentleman like Wesley Pruiss who wants to do something about the energy crisis and we're all proud to be helping him and playing a part. This is America,

11

you know, or maybe you don't, because we hear what goes on there in New York City, fella.

The combined bands of Furlong County High School, St. Luke's High School, Lincoln Junior High School, Ettinger Junior High and the police and fire marching society were playing when Wesley Pruiss arrived in Furlong.

He was with Theodosia. He introduced her as his secretary. She wore a white cotton top and matching houri trousers and the sun behind her made them transparent.

One woman in the crowd looked at Pruiss and said, "He don't look like no perverter, Melvin."

"Who?" said Melvin, staring at Theodosia and gulping a lot.

Wesley Pruiss said he was happy to be among his people. The band played some more. It kept playing as Pruiss and Theodosia left the airport.

Pruiss had already decided that the only building in the county that he would consider spending a night in was the Furlong Country Club, so he closed down the golf course and took it over as his home.

The bands lined up alongside the practice putting green as Pruiss and Theodosia went inside. They played "Hail to the Chief" a lot. Pruiss told them to go home. They cheered and played some more.

Pruiss told them he loved them all.

The audience cheered. The band played "Hail to the Chief."

Pruiss told the crowd that they must have more important things to do than just greet him.

They shook their heads and cheered. The band played "Garryowen."

"And now I am weary and must sleep," Pruiss said, working hard at keeping his smile.

"We'll play soft," the bandleader shouted. He raised his hands to put the bands into Brahms's Lullaby.

"Get the fuck out of here!" Pruiss screamed.

The longer he had been away from the Jersey City slum he grew up in, the more golden it had grown in Wesley Pruiss's memory. He had invested the town with some kind of mythic quality, an ability to create toughness and smarts, which he credited for his success in the world.

In talking to the press, Pruiss always referred to himself as a street kid, a slum kid, a kid who learned to fight almost as soon as he learned to walk. A kid who had to fight to survive. He gave bonuses to members of the *Gross* public relations staff who could get that point of view into any national publication. He relished reading about himself as the tough urchin, the child of the streets.

Across the street from the Furlong Country Club, there was a small cluster of three-story frame buildings. One of them looked to Pruiss a little like the cold-water tenement building in which he had been raised in Jersey City. He sent for an architect.

When he explained his idea, the architect said: "You sure you want to do this?"

"Just do it," Pruiss said.

"It'll cost a lot of money."

"Do it."

"You really want me to import garbage and break windows and throw rubble in those lots?" the architect asked.

"That's right."

"You could do it a lot cheaper by starting an affirmative-action housing program," the architect said.

13

"Those people litter a lot faster than workmen on an eight-hour shift."

"That's all right," Pruiss said. "I'm interested in quality, not quantity. You do it."

The architect tore down the two end buildings in a three-building cluster. He showed up with contractors and plans and took the structurally-sound, neat, three-story building and turned it into a six-family cold-water walkup. He grumbled a lot and refused to let his name be used in any promotion Pruiss might do about the building.

Every day, as his little transplanted slum area took shape, Pruiss looked from the window of his bedroom, which used to be the country club's card room, and nodded approvingly.

It was done in two weeks.

"You want to inspect it?" the architect said.

"You did it just the way you were supposed to?"

The architect nodded.

"It looks just like the building in Jersey City?" Pruiss asked.

"Exactly. God help me."

"Fine. Send your bill to Theodosia. She'll pay you right away."

That night, there was a full moon over Furlong County. Theodosia was downstairs in the country club's suite of offices, working on Pruiss's personal profit and loss statements.

Pruiss looked out his bedroom window and the top of the three-story building across the street was bathed in a soft white moonglow. He put a light sweater over his T-shirt and walked across the street.

As he stepped inside the door of the replicated tenement, his palms began to sweat.

He looked up the steps. There was a bare bulb

burning at the top of the second-floor landing. It cast long shadows down along the wooden steps, each stair meticulously swaybacked in the center, duplicating tenement steps curved and bowed from years of being walked on in the center. Pruiss stepped on the first stair. It squeaked, as it always had when he was a boy. The smell of urine in the hall was strong and bitter.

Sweat broke out on Pruiss's forehead.

He was frightened, just as he had always been frightened, every time he walked up the stairs of that building, the bare wooden steps that led to hallways lined with green linoleum, worn through in spots, installed in a desperate and futile attempt to make the building cheery.

For all his talk of being a child of the streets, the streets had terrified Pruiss. He was smaller than other boys his age and they didn't like him, and whereas they seemed not to mind living in dangerous, dirty slums, Pruiss was frightened for his life every moment of his childhood. It was as if he alone, of all the boys, knew how impermanent life was and that his life was precious, something to be guarded. He had taken to spending more and more time in the family's apartment with his hardworking mother and rarely-seen father, dreaming of what life would be like when he was grown and powerful and rich.

Both mother and father were gone now. He wished they had been around to see him make it.

The farther he walked up the steps, the more he perspired. The light over the third floor landing was out, as it always had been when he was a boy. He forced himself to go upstairs, knowing even as he did it that it was a mistake, something he should not do, something he should never do. The perspiration rolled off his head. There were crumpled-up newspapers and a crushed brown paper bag in one corner of the hallway. That was where Mr. Bailey, who lived one flight down, always disposed of the evidence of the bottle of wine he brought home and hid in his apartment. Outside one of the apartment doors, a stack of newspapers was piled neatly and tied. Those were Mrs. Acalara's papers. She was a widow and Wesley would carry her papers to the junkyard down the block on the back of his wagon. He always went very early on Saturday morning when the big kids weren't out yet. A three-foot high pile of papers would sell for twenty cents. Mrs. Acalara always gave him a nickel to keep for himself.

Pruiss stood in the darkness of the third floor landing and listened to the stillness of the building. There was no sound except for his breathing and his heartbeat thumping in his ears.

He had never been so frightened in his life. It was as if he had walked through a time warp into the past. He put his hand on the doorknob to the Pruiss family's flat. He told himself that he was rich and powerful now and this was no longer a rundown building in a strange tough city where he had been just another potential victim. This was his building in his town, his county, his piece of the world. And he was king.

He swallowed hard, took a deep breath and opened the door and stepped inside. He reached for the overhead light string just inside the door and pulled it but there was no answer of lights. In his childhood, there had hardly ever been, for old man Pruiss was not among the world's most consistent or productive workers and the electric bill had rarely been paid.

16

Wesley Pruiss had been brought up in the dim light and the bitter smoky smell of kerosene lamps.

He reached in his pants for a Butane lighter. In the dim moonlight through a kitchen window, he could see the kerosene lamp on top of the red and white oil-cloth covering the kitchen table. The table underneath, he knew, was porcelain topped metal, with chips in the porcelain at the corners where the bare metal showed through.

The kitchen was redolent with the enduring smell of poverty, of cabbage, of kidney and liver. He looked toward the sink. There was a gauzy bag of white stuff hanging from the old fashioned faucet. That would be a bag of curdled milk, dripping away its juices, being turned into pot cheese by the necessarily-frugal Mrs. Pruiss.

He struck the lighter and reached for the kerosene lamp.

A voice behind him said, "I've been waiting for you."

Pruiss dropped the lighter. It went out, hit the table and fell onto the floor.

He whirled and looked into the darkness of the passageway leading to the apartment's living room.

"Who's there?"

There was no answer. Pruiss was still, but all he could hear was his breathing and the thumping of his pulse.

"I said who's there?"

His answer was silence, and Pruiss wheeled back and dropped to the floor, wiping it with his hand, looking for the cigarette lighter.

He heard a whirring sound behind him. Then he felt something bite into his back and although it was something outside his experience, he knew as he felt

17

it force its way into his flesh that it was the blade of a knife that had been thrown at him.

Then the feeling left his legs and Wesley Pruiss sank slowly forward onto his face on the floor and he knew that something bad had happened to his body, something very bad, and the pain of the knife in his back was like a heated spear, but then the spear seemed to cool and Wesley Pruiss found that he could close his eyes and sleep.

But as he lapsed into unconsciousness, a thought came into his mind with bright, searing clarity. The thought was that even if he had done some bad things, he did not deserve a knife in the back. That was unjust, and if there was such a thing as justice, there should be justice even for those who do bad. His last thought as he closed his eyes was, Is there no one who can give me justice?

CHAPTER TWO

His name was Remo and he knew what justice was.
Justice was time-and-a-half for overtime. Justice was
not being given more jobs in a night than you could
reasonably handle. Justice was being appreciated for
what you did better than anyone else.

All those things were justice and Remo knew there
was no justice.

So he knew the man he wanted would not be
where Upstairs said he would be, and he resigned
himself to having to trail him all over New York, finally winding up in some strobe-lighted disco whose
sound level would turn sand to glass.

Remo slid into the empty seat at the small round-
topped table and Kenroth Winstler looked up at him
with a bemused smile on his face. The man sitting
across from Winstler was certainly dressed strangely
for a discotheque, even in an age of wrinkled cottons
and baggy jumpsuits. The man wore black chinos and
a black T-shirt. He had dark hair and deep-set eyes
that were like pools of night and he seemed slim, ex-

19

cept for thick wrists that he rested on the table. He looked at Winstler for a long time as if making sure of something.

"I'm sorry, Mr." Winstler said, nodding toward Remo and the chair he occupied. "But I'm expecting a lady."

"That's all right," Remo said. "I'll be gone and you'll be dead before she gets here. My name's Remo, by the way."

Winstler smiled. The din from the disco records was deafening. If he hadn't known better, he would have sworn that the man opposite him was saying that Kenroth Winstler was going to die.

"I'm sorry, I didn't hear you," Winstler said.

"You heard me," Remo said. "Now I've got a lot of things to do tonight and not much time to waste, so just tell me, please, where is the Red Regiment?"

Winstler leaned forward to hear him better. He thought the man had asked him where the Red Regiment was.

"What?"

"Are you going to keep answering my questions with questions?" Remo said. He mouthed the words carefully and slowly. "The . . . Red . . . Regiment . . . Where?"

Winstler heard him clearly this time and turned around, looking for a waiter to throw the man out.

"That's all right," Remo said. "I don't want anything. Well, maybe a glass of water. No, never mind. In this place, water would curdle."

Winstler ignored him and kept looking for a waiter. Remo sighed. He slid his chair around next to Winstler's. Winstler saw the waiter in the back of the room. He was about to wave to him, when he felt a bitter pain in his right knee, a pain so intense that it felt as if his knee were being cut into by a dull and rusty saw. He turned away, the waiter forgotten, and clapped his hand to his right knee. His hand landed on Remo's hand. Remo's face was close to his now and Remo was smiling.

"See," Remo said. "That's pain. Now if you don't want pain, we're going to talk nicey-nice. I told you already, I don't have a lot of time."

Winstler had no trouble hearing the thin young man now. The pain in his knee subsided briefly.

"Where's the Red Regiment holed up?" asked Remo.

"Did you say before you were going to kill me?" Winstler asked.

"See. There you go again. Asking questions instead of just answering." The pain returned to the knee. Winstler grimaced. He would have screamed except Remo's left hand had come around his back and was resting on his left shoulder and one finger was touching something in Winstler's throat and no sound came out.

"Yes, of course I'm going to kill you," Remo said.

"Why?" gasped Winstler.

"Now, you might reasonably think," Remo said, "that it's because you always answer a question with a question. But that's not the reason. I'm going to kill you because that's what I do. And do. And do. No one cares how much I work. No unions for me. If I ever get in a deal like this again, I'm getting me a lawyer, a fancy lawyer like you. Now, come on, the Red Regiment, where are they?"

Winstler hesitated and there was the pain again in the knee. He tried to scream and there was the finger again alongside the throat. The throat pressure lessened.

21

"I don't know," he gasped.

"Aww, come on," Remo said in annoyance. "What do you lawyers say, that's not responsive. You know and I know that you know and I've got to find out so I can go there and get that businessman they're holding free and now will you please tell me 'cause it's getting late and I've got a lot of things to do."

"What makes you think I know?" Winstler tried again.

"Because they're loonies and you defend all the loonies and besides your secretary's been dropping a dime on you all the while and letting Upstairs know who you talk to on the phone. And you been talking to the Red Regiment, so come on."

And then there was the pain again, but this time it was pointed, shafting pain. Winstler felt tears come to his eyes. It felt as if his kneecap had rusted onto his leg and this man was wrenching it free.

"See, real pain is like that," Remo said.

"You're really going to kill me." This time it was not a question. For the first time, Winstler believed that perhaps this man might mean what he had said. "Here? In this disco?"

"Why not? For supporting music like this, you deserve death. Where are they?"

"If I tell you, you let me live."

"No," Remo said.

"Why not?"

"Because I'm going to kill you whether you tell me or not," Remo said.

"Then why should I tell you?"

"Why not out of an overriding commitment to the truth, above all things?" Remo said. Winstler shook his head. "All right," Remo said. "Because of this. There are lots of ways to die. There are quick and

22

painless ways and there are slow and painful ways and they only make you want the quick and painless ways. Now it's up to you. I only have five more minutes."

"Let me live," Winstler said.

The waiter appeared alongside the table. Winstler felt the slight thumb pressure on his throat again and his voice vanished.

"Would you care for something?" the waiter asked, looking at Winstler and ignoring the man in the black T-shirt.

"Yes, some privacy," Remo said. "Can't you see we're talking? Get out of here."

The waiter sniffed and walked away.

The pressure softened on the throat.

"Let me live," Winstler said.

"No. Absolutely not," Remo said.

"Let me live and I'll give you the Red Regiment. And I'll give you those saloon bombers in New York and the Pan-Palestinian skyjackers."

"I don't want them," Remo said.

"Why not?"

"Because I've got enough to do. I'm not volunteering for anything. The Red Regiment."

There was the pain again in the knee, this time even sharper than before and Winstler quickly blurted out an address in the east seventies. Lights from the disco Strobe-n-Globe flashed across his face and Remo saw panic in his eyes.

"And the guy they kidnaped is there too?" Remo asked. He had to speak up to be heard over the screech of the music.

"Right, right."

"Good," Remo said.

"You're still going to kill me?"

"Of course."

"But why? Who are you anyway? To come in here and talk about killing?"

"Just another overworked wage slave," Remo said.

"But who?" Winstler asked again.

"It's a long story," Remo said.

"I've got time," Winstler said. If he could get his knee free, he could bolt from the table. In the crush of bodies on the dance floor he'd be safe.

"No, you haven't," Remo said. "All right, three minutes. See, there was this cop in Newark, New Jersey. His name was Remo Williams. That was me. He got framed for a murder he didn't do and got sent to an electric chair that didn't work and then he woke up after everybody thought he was dead and they put him to work for a secret government organization. It's called CURE."

"What do they do?" Winstler asked. The grip was still a vise on his right knee.

"What do they do? They give a guy more work than he can possibly handle. Next thing they'll be handing me a broom for my butt so I can sweep the streets on my way."

"Besides overworking you," Winstler said.

"Yeah. Well, this organization works outside the Constitution to take care of people that hide behind the Constitution. Criminals. Troublemakers. Like that. People like you. We preserve the Constitution by violating it, in a way."

"And what do you do?" Winstler asked. "Remo Williams?"

"Right. Remo Williams. I'm the assassin. The only one. Of course, there's Chiun and he's an assassin too.

"That's fascistic," Winstler said.

"Sounds about right," Remo said agreeably. "Any-

24

way, it shouldn't surprise you. You've been saying that for years. Even when I was a cop, I read about you. You were always calling America a fascist state."

"That didn't mean I believed it," the lawyer said. He was hoping. If he could keep this Remo talking, he might just stay alive. He remembered an old story about a court magician who fell out of favor with his king and was sentenced to death.

"Too bad," the magician told the king. "I was just going to teach your horse to fly."

Upon hearing that, the king lifted the death penalty and gave the magician a year to teach the horse to fly.

That night, a friend asked the magician why he had said that to the king. "A horse can't fly," he said. "Why'd you do it?"

"A lot of things can happen in a year," the magician said. "I might die. The king might die. Or, who knows. I might just teach that goddamn horse how to fly."

If he could only keep this Remo talking, he might yet be able to escape with his life.

"Time's up," Remo said. "I've got to go now."

"You can't just come in here and kill me," Winstler said. "It's not . . . it's not right."

"I don't want to hear about that," Remo said. "Everybody's always telling me what I can and can't do. I'm tired of that."

"But you can't. You can't just kill me."

Remo leaned closer and smiled at Kenroth Winstler. "You know what?" he asked.

"What?"

"I just did," Remo said.

The fingertips pressing into the kidney were so fast that Winstler never really felt pain. Remo wiped his right hand on the table cloth and stood up. He let Winstler's head slump forward softly on the table cloth and walked away.

Fascist, Winstler had called him. That annoyed him and Remo didn't believe it for a minute. Fascist. If it weren't for lawyers like Winstler who spent so much time and effort and other people's money getting criminals off, there would be no need for Remo and people like him. He wished he had not killed Winstler so fast, so he could tell him that.

Fascist? Remo? It was laughable.

He still wished he could remember something else he was supposed to do that night. It nagged at him.

On his way out, he tapped the waiter on the shoulder.

"Yes sir," the waiter said as he turned. He recognized Remo and his eyes frosted over. "What is it?" he said.

"That man at my table?" Remo said.

"Yes. Mr. Winstler."

"Well, he's dead."

"What?" the waiter said. His eyes peered toward the table where Winstler slumped forward, his hands under his face.

"I said dead," Remo said again. "I killed him. And if you don't do something about this noise in here, I'm coming back for you."

The waiter looked away from the table to Remo. But the thin man in the black T-shirt was gone. The waiter looked around, into the crowd, but saw no sign of him. It was as if the earth had opened and swallowed him up.

Downstairs at the party, they had only marijuana, and speed and LSD and snow and horse and fairy

26

princess and HTC and amyl nitrate and aspirins in Coke and opium lettuce and Acapulco Gold and Tijuana Small and Kent Golden Lights so it was really a drag and Marcia went up on the roof with Jeffrey because he had some good shit and he didn't have enough to share with everybody else.

On the roof of the small apartment building in the east seventies, they unwrapped the package of Lightning Dust, following the careful directions Jeffrey had been given along with the drug by a guru with an eighth-grade education that qualified him to be a spokesman for the eternal power of the universe, which meant drug dealing.

They had to inhale a puff of the powder through the left nostril and exhale their breath through the right nostril. Then they had to inhale through the right nostril and exhale through the left nostril. Then, while humming their mantra, just hard enough for their vocal cords to vibrate, they had to touch their tongue to the powder on the small square of paper, wet it with saliva, swallow it down, and then lie back to wait for ecstasy.

The exact sequence was very important, Jeffrey had been told. They followed it precisely, then lay on the sharp-pebbled roof, waiting for bliss. It was longer in coming than they expected, which was not surprising because Jeffrey had spent sixty dollars for a quarter ounce of powdered milk, mixed one-to-one with powdered vitamin C. Its total cost to the dealer had been three-tenths of a cent. Its caloric content was higher than that.

Jeffrey interlocked his fingers with Marcia who lay alongside him, then closed his eyes. When he opened them again, the stars were still shining brightly in the dark night sky. He glanced from side to side. Nothing. He had been promised light shows and sonic booms and celestial pyrotechnics, but nothing.

"You getting it yet?" he asked Marcia.

"I don't know," she said. "I don't think so. Everything's the same."

They raised themselves into a sitting position, propped against the brick wall around the roof, and tried another dose. Left nostril, right nostril, tongue, saliva, swallow.

And then they saw it.

A man came over the wall of the roof, as if he had climbed up the side of the building. He was a thin man, dressed in black T-shirt and chinos and his eyes were dark and his hair was dark and his wrists were thick. As he moved across the roof, he nodded to them.

"Just keep doing whatever it is you're doing," he said. "I won't be but a few minutes."

Then he vanished over the far wall of the roof, and Jeffrey and Marcia looked at each other with surprise on their faces.

"There's no fire escape there," Jeffrey said.

"I know," Marcia said. "Wow."

They went to the edge of the roof where the man had disappeared. When they looked down, he was going down the smooth side of the brick building, as easily as if he were walking down a ladder. But there was no ladder and no fire escape.

"How you doing that, fella?" Marcia called. "Going down like that and all?"

"Shhhh," Remo called up. "It's an optical illusion. Actually, I'm staying still and you're going up."

"Hey, wow," Marcia said. "Jeff, you got any more of that?"

They sniffed and salivaed and swallowed and kept watching but they were quiet.

Remo would have preferred it if they had gone away because he didn't like performing in front of witnesses, but he didn't have much choice. And besides he had a problem.

There was a window about ten feet away that led into the apartment where the Red Regiment was holed up. If he went through the window, they might be able to kill the businessman before he could rescue him. That was why he had not gone through the apartment's front door. He not only had to get into the apartment quickly, but shockingly enough to stun the Red Regiment so it had no chance to react.

As Jeffrey and Marcia finished their new sniff of powdered milk and vitamin C, Jeffrey looked up to the sky, but the stars were still dully immobile.

"Nothing with the stars," he said. "Maybe this stuff only works with your perception of people."

Marcia nodded. She had not been able to take her eyes off the thin man since he had crossed the rooftop. There was something about his eyes and the way he moved, something that made her know that he could make her forget every other man in the world. She watched the apparition hang to the side of the building. He was holding onto the smooth brick with his left hand, with no more effort than if he had been leaning against the wall of an elevator. His right fingertips were being driven into the building.

"Look," she hissed. "He's pulling bricks out of the building."

Jeffrey looked down. One by one, Remo was removing bricks from the wall and dropping them down into the small dirty yard behind the old apartment building.

"How's he doing that?" she said.

Jeffrey's voice was thick. "Gotta remember," he said. "He's not doing nothing. Our heads are doing it. He ain't really there. We're here. We make him there in our heads. If we close our eyes and want him to go away, when we open our eyes, he'll go away."

Marcia tried it. She closed her eyes, squinted them together real hard, then opened them. Remo was still tossing bricks into the yard, making a hole in the building wall.

"Whooops," she said. She was happy he was still there.

Jeffrey had tried also. "Gotta practice some more," he said. "This stuff's not easy to use."

"How you doin' that?" Marcia yelled at Remo.

"I'm not doing it," he called back. "Actually I'm staying still and you and the building are moving backwards. Have some more grass."

"This isn't grass. It's Lightning Dust. Wanna come up and make it with me?"

"Later," Remo said. "Soon as I'm done."

"All right," Marcia said. "I'll wait."

Remo had the hole big enough now. The two-by-fours of the interior walls and the lathing strips and the rough inside surface of the wall plaster were clearly visible.

Jeffrey was looking at the sky, hoping for an aurora borealis.

"Hey, Jeffy, look," Marcia said.

Jeffrey leaned over and looked but all he saw was a pile of bricks in the yard.

"What?" he said.

"He jus' go through that wall. Like it isn't there," Marcia said. She giggled. Jeffrey leaned over to try to see better. As they both watched, a body soared through the hole in the rear wall and out into the yard where it hit the bricks with a wet, doughy thump and lay still. They heard a thwacking sound, and another body came flying through the hole into the yard. Then more sounds and another body and another. They all hit hard. Two of them bounced on contact. None of them moved afterward.

"Wow," Marcia said.

"You can say that again."

"Wow," said Marcia who thought it was stupid to say it again.

"I'm gonna see the guru tomorrow and get us some more of this," Jeffrey said.

Marcia didn't answer. She was waiting for the man in black to come back out of the hole in the brick wall and climb up to the roof and make love to her. And if he had to fight off Jeffrey, so much the better. And if he couldn't fight off Jeffrey, then she would fight off Jeffrey.

But Remo didn't come.

He found the kidnaped businessman in a closet, blindfolded, gagged and tied. Remo removed the gag and the ropes, but left the man's blindfold on.

"You're all right now," he said.

"Who are you?"

"Just another guy trying to do two men's work," Remo said.

The hostage reached for his blindfold but Remo stayed his hand.

"You can take that off when you hear the front door close," he said.

"Where are they?" the businessman asked.

"They left," Remo said.

"I heard noises. Like a fight."

"No, there wasn't any fight," Remo said truthfully.

31

"Some scurrying, maybe, but no fight. Look, I'm going now. You take that off when I leave."

On the roof, three minutes had passed and Marcia had decided that that was long enough to wait for the one great love in her life. She would live with the tragedy forever, the sense of loss that the man in black had not come back. She would suffer. She would even give her body to Jeffrey out of her sense of remorse. She would try to find happiness in the arms of many lovers.

"Jeffrey," she said. "I'm yours. Take me."

She turned to look for Jeffrey. He was sleeping in a corner of the roof, snoring heavily. Marcia thought about it for a moment, then lay down beside him. She would give her body away tomorrow, to try to drown her sorrows in the arms of many men. But for now she would sleep.

Remo got a cab on the corner and told the driver he was in a hurry to get to Brooklyn.

"How much of a hurry?"

"A hundred dollar hurry," Remo said, flashing the bill at the driver.

"How much of a tip?"

"That includes the tip," Remo said.

"Okay. You're as good as there. Did you hear about . . ."

Remo touched the driver on the right shoulder.

"I also want it quiet. I'm trying to think of something. So every time you say anything from here on in, I'm taking ten dollars off the hundred."

"All right. I won't say a word," the driver said.

"That's ninety," Remo said.

The driver wouldn't make that mistake again. Ninety dollars to Brooklyn was all right and everybody knew that New York cab drivers were the smartest in the world, so he decided he would say nothing, not a word, he would just let that hundred dollar looney sit in silence, but there was that shine who looked like he might be going to cut him off and put a dent in the last unscarred spot on his left front fender and that was worth a yell, and hell, everybody wanted to hear some kind of comment on New York's weather, and the passenger must have an opinion about the New York Yankees, and maybe the passenger would like to see his polished rock collection because sometimes people bought rocks from him and a man who would pay a hundred dollars to get to Brooklyn might pay God knows how much for rocks that the driver got himself at this little place called Snake Hill, across the river in Secaucus, New Jersey, and by and by they reached Brooklyn and Remo hadn't had any chance at all to think and at ten dollars deduction per outburst, the driver owed Remo forty dollars.

He did not want to pay.

Remo extracted it from the man's pocket.

"If you want to wait," he said, "I'll give you the same deal going back."

"Hell, no," the driver said. "You think I'm made of forty dollarses?" He jammed the car into gear and drove off angrily, scratching the last virgin piece of fender on a heavy wire trash basket used by the neighborhood as a Dempster dumpster.

The building on Halsey Street was a tired, chalky old tenement. Outlined against the black midnight sky, with no lights on, it looked like dirt rampant on a field of dirt. Remo double-checked the address. This was it. The basement.

He went down the stairs in the back of the first

floor hall. The cellar was dark but he moved easily between the ash cans and the stacks of newspaper to the locked door in the rear of the cellar. The old wooden door fit in its frame so tightly that no leak of light showed around its edges. He touched his fingertips to the wood and could feel the heat from inside that signified a light on.

Good. It was getting late and Remo wanted to be finished with this day.

Remo reached his hands up above his head, then drove the fingertips of his arched hands into the wood. They slammed in like nail punches. Remo yanked the door toward him, the lock snapped and the door came off the hinges easily. Remo tossed it to the side.

A big man was working at a bench. He was wearing boxer shorts and an undershirt. A heavy mat of hair covered his shoulders. He whirled toward Remo.

"What the . . ."

"Not a lot of time," Remo said. "You Ernie Bombarelli?"

"Yeah," the man growled. "Who the hell . . ."

Remo silenced him with a wave of his hand.

"Nice factory you've got here," he said. He looked around at the neat cans of powder and the long waxed cardboard tubes. "You could win a war with all these explosives."

"I could punch your face out, creep. Who are you?"

"You've been pushing these firecrackers in schoolyards. Last week, two kids lost their hands playing with your toys."

"I don't know nothin' about that," Bombarelli said.

"One of the kids was a concert piano player," Remo said.

Bombarelli shrugged. "Maybe he can learn to play with his feet."

"I'm glad you said that," Remo said.

Bombarelli's right hand was easing behind his back, toward a small drawer in the end of the workbench.

"Don't waste my time with guns," Remo said. "It won't do any good."

It didn't. Bombarelli had the gun out and in his hand and pointed at the skinny intruder. He squeezed the trigger but the gun never went off and then it was in the skinny guy's hands and then with two hands he snapped the gun apart and dropped the pieces onto the concrete cellar floor.

"Who . . ." Bombarelli started again.

"Who doesn't matter," Remo said. "What matters is that this is the kind of work I do. Every so often, I just get somebody who's a piece of garbage like you and fix him up so that he's kind of a lesson to the other pieces of garbage. It's your turn in the barrel, Bombarelli."

Bombarelli went for Remo's throat with his hands. He was a big man, with shoulders like the hams of a champion hog, but Remo met the hands with his own hands, and squeezed his thumbs into the inside of Bombarelli's wrists, and the firecracker manufacturer's fingers didn't work any more. He tried to yell, but there was another thumb in his throat and he couldn't yell. He tried to run, but there was a thumb in the base of his spine and his legs didn't work, not even to hold him up, and Ernie Bombarelli crumpled onto the cellar floor. All that worked were his eyes and they worked too well because as Bombarelli watched in growing horror, the thin man began scooping up M-80s from the work-bench, firecrackers almost three inches long and an inch-and-a-half thick, and with

35

tape, he began fastening them to Bombarelli's thick, hairy fingers.

"No," Bombarelli tried to say but no sound came.

The only sound in the cellar was the thin man in the black shirt and the black chinos. He was softly whistling. He was whistling "Whistle While You Work."

He put a cluster of the lethal firecrackers around Bombarelli's neck and fastened them with tape. Then the looney had a piece of fuse, a long piece, and he was twisting it around the other fuses, wrapping it around the firecrackers, each of them the power of a third of a stick of dynamite, and he still whistled and smiled down at Bombarelli.

"Don't think about it, Bombarelli," he said. "There's no real why. It's just that every so often I do one like you. Kind of a Bum of the Month club." Remo dragged the fuse toward the cellar door. He dropped it on the floor and looked around in his pockets for a match. But he did not have one and came back to get one off the work bench, stepping casually over Bombarelli's body as he did.

"So long, Bombarelli," Remo said, as he struck a match and lit the long length of fuse. Then he was gone out into the darkness of the cellar. Bombarelli did not hear his footsteps going up the steps to the first floor, but he knew the man was leaving. All he could think of was the spark of the fuse, creeping its hissing way across the floor toward him, closer, closer, five feet, then four feet, then three feet, then closer and only inches, and then he heard the first blast and felt the heat, and then there was blast after blast, but the first one had provided all the pain to Bombarelli that his living body could register, and then the rest of the explosives went off and the cellar exploded in a flash of flame.

There was a cab stopped for a red light at the corner of Halsey Street. Remo waved at the cab. The cabbie pointed to his roof light; it was off, indicating that he was off-duty. Remo pulled open the locked door anyway.

"Hey," the driver said. "I'm off-duty."

"So am I," Remo said. "A hundred dollars if you get me to Manhattan without talking."

"Let's see the hundred."

Remo held it up.

"Okay. On to Manhattan," the driver said.

Remo nodded.

"How'd you open the door? It was locked."

"That's ninety," Remo said with a sigh.

Even though it was past midnight, Chiun was waiting for Remo when he entered the hotel room two blocks from New York's Central Park. The aged, wizened Korean sat in his blue kimono on a straw mat, staring at the door, as if he had waited there for hours for Remo's return.

"Did you bring them?" he asked. His voice was a high squeak with only two gears. Its range went from annoyance to outrage, with no steps in between.

"Bring what them?" Remo asked.

"I knew it," Chiun hissed. "I send you on a simple errand and you forget even what the errand was."

Remo snapped his fingers. "The chestnuts. I'm sorry, I forgot."

" 'I'm sorry. I forgot,' " Chiun mimicked. "I do not pay you to forget."

"You don't pay me at all, Little Father," Remo said.

"There are payments other than money," Chiun

said. "All I ask for is a chestnut. A simple roasted chestnut."

"You asked for a pound, as I remember," Remo said.

"*Now* you remember. Just a few roasted chestnuts. To remind me of my childhood in the ancient village of Sinanju. And what do I get? 'I'm sorry. I forgot.' Remo, why do you think I even bother to come to this ugly city, except that they have chestnuts for sale on the street?"

"I'm sorry, already. Get off it. I'll get them tomorrow. All the chestnut salesmen have gone home by now and I had other things to do besides shop for you."

"If you really wanted to help, you would find where one lives and go there and get my chestnuts," Chiun said. He paused. "Your breathing was not correct tonight."

"How can you tell? It wasn't all that off."

"It does not have to be 'all that off,'" Chiun said. "The fall to death does not start with a dive. It starts with a slip."

Remo shrugged. "So the breathing wasn't perfect. You're not going to make me feel bad. I did some good things tonight."

"Oh?"

"Yes," Remo said.

"Did you send money to the poor and sick of my village?"

"No."

"Did you buy me some trinket to show your love for me?"

"No."

"I have it," Chiun said. He allowed his face to smile. It looked like a book, covered in yellow parchment, suddenly being opened. "Actually, you purchased for me the chestnuts and you are teasing me."

"No," Remo said.

"Pfaaaah," Chiun squeaked, turning away from Remo in disgust.

"I got rid of a lawyer who fronts for criminals. I freed a kidnap victim from a gang of revolutionary goons. And I got rid of a guy who peddles dangerous explosives to kids."

"And you call this good?" Chiun demanded. "Good is when you do something that helps the Master of Sinanju. That is good. Good is bringing me my simple chestnut. That is good. Bringing me Barbra Streisand would be even better but I would settle for a chestnut. Bringing gold and diamonds for my village is good. That is good. And what do you tell me is good? Something about a lawyer and a gang and a man who makes booms."

"Bombs," Remo said. "And getting rid of them was good and I don't care what you say."

"I know that," Chiun said. "That is exactly what is wrong with you."

"What I did was good and that means something, Chiun, and you know it. I used to think that what I did with CURE would improve America, then for a long time I didn't think it did. But it does. Maybe not the way I figured. Maybe I'm not going to stamp out crime and terrorism, but I'm stamping out some criminals and some terrorists and that's the next best thing. Not many people can claim to do even that much good."

"What you think is good is moral nonsense," Chiun said. "Chestnuts are good. Moving correctly is good. Not being sloppy is good. Breathing correctly is good. What does it matter who you practice on?"

Before Remo could answer, the telephone rang.

"That is Smith," Chiun said.

"He call before?"

"I presume so. Somebody called. But I do not answer telephones. Then a bell person came with a message and it was from Smith and said that he would call again."

"Thanks for the warning," Remo said.

He reached for the phone again.

"Remo?" Chiun said.

Remo turned. The old Oriental was smiling.

"Yes, Little Father," Remo said.

"If Smith is coming here, tell him to bring chestnuts."

CHAPTER THREE

Dr. Harold W. Smith's face exuded all the natural charm and sweetness of a clam. It was pinched and tight around the mouth and his eyes were cold and unblinking. His natural expression was lemon twist and if he had been older, he would remind people of the original John D. Rockefeller. Except, unlike Rockefeller, Harold W. Smith would never give away dimes to the starving poor. In a fit of rampant good will, he might have tried to find them jobs—working for somebody else.

He could make the overseer of a Peruvian tin mine look warm. He looked like the kind of man you would want representing you if you were trying to negotiate a contract with a publisher.

He sat in a straight-backed chair in the hotel room, facing Remo. Smith's gray suit was immaculately pressed and unwrinkled, as if it had been built out of fiberglass in a custom auto body shop. His shirt collar seemed a half size too small and was buttoned tightly, and the points were heavily starched. His Dartmouth regimental tie was so stiff it seemed made of ceramic.

Remo sat on the bed. Chiun was in the corner of the room, on his grass mat, sitting lightly in a lotus position, smilingly attacking a bagful of roasted chestnuts that Smith had brought with him. Chiun's technique was to grab the bottom of the chestnut between two long-nailed fingers and squeeze. The kernel of the nut popped up through the top.

"How did you find us?" Remo asked. "We're not in our regular hotel."

Smith sniffed. "I don't suppose there are too many people in the area registered as 'Remo and Glorious One.'" He nodded toward Chiun, who froze his chestnut-bearing hand on its way toward his mouth.

"I told Remo we should use a different hotel, Emperor," said Chiun. "I saw no reason in our spending so much of your money at that other hotel with the high ceilings, particularly when I know you have only so much money and so many demands on it."

Remo smiled. Chiun being concerned about Smith's budget problems could be nothing but the first step in negotiations for a pay raise.

Chiun chewed the chestnut. "How much were these chestnuts?" he asked.

Smith waved a hand in dismissal.

"No," Chiun protested. "I insist upon paying for them. I think a man should pay for what he gets. I should pay for these chestnuts. I would expect that if I were working for someone, he would pay me what I was worth. How much were they? I insist, Emperor."

"All right," Smith said. "A dollar."

"Remo," said Chiun. "Give the Emperor a dollar."

When Remo's hand did not move instantly for his

pocket, Chiun said again, more loudly: "Remo. A dollar for Emperor Smith."

Remo reluctantly fished a roll of bills from his pocket and flicked through it, riffling the corners of the bills as if they were a deck of playing cards.

"Nothing smaller than a five, Smitty. You got change?"

Smith reached for the five. "No," he said. "I'll owe you four."

Remo put the bills back in his pocket. "Never mind," he said. "I'll owe you one."

"I will make sure he pays it," Chiun said. "Because I believe a man should always pay for what he gets. This is the way the House of Sinanju has always behaved." The chestnuts were gone now and Chiun pushed aside the empty bag as if it contained something distasteful.

Smith looked at Chiun, a hard look, and then said blandly: "Ruby Gonzalez is in charge of all salary negotiations from now on."

Chiun's face turned sour.

"Who?"

"Ruby Gonzalez," Smith said.

"This is cruel and unkind," Chiun said. "There is no talking to that woman."

Remo laughed. To watch Ruby, the beautiful street-smart black woman who was now Smith's assistant, engaged in contract negotiations with Chiun would be an event you could sell tickets for.

"Where *is* Ruby?" Remo asked.

"On vacation," Smith said.

"I figured that," Remo said.

"Why?"

"Because for the past week it's been nothing but work, work, work. Ruby's a pain in the butt and her voice sounds like glass breaking but she has the good sense to space out jobs for me," Remo said. "You just keep piling them on one after the other."

"I will have to speak to Ruby about that," Smith said drily. He fished in his leather briefcase, once tan but turned brown through decades of exposure to wind, rain and sun, and brought out a TV tape cassette.

"Could I have the television player, please?" he asked.

"Chiun, do we still have the tape player?" Remo asked. At one time, they would have travelled nowhere without it because it was the only way Chiun could manage to keep up with what was happening every day on every soap opera. But then the television soaps became "realistic," which Chiun equated with dirty, and he stopped watching them.

Chiun pointed to one of the fourteen lacquered steamer trunks that lined the walls of the hotel room and contained his "few personal possessions."

"It is in there," he said. "I never throw away anything the Emperor has paid for. I will get it."

He rose like a cloud drifting into the air, opened the top of the trunk and bent down into it. His tiny body seemed almost to vanish into the trunk, like a child bent over a tub, bobbing for Halloween apples.

He finally came out with the TV machine, lifting the heavy instrument with no more effort than if it had been a one-page letter from home.

It nearly dropped from Smith's hands as Chiun gave it to him. Smith lugged it over to the television set, efficiently hooked it into the back of the set, and then inserted the cassette into the top.

"Good," said Chiun. "A show. I have not seen a good show in much time."

The TV tape began rolling and the picture came on the screen.

It was a picture of Wesley Pruiss in a hospital bed, his face wan and drawn, crisp white sheets pulled up to his neck.

"Good," Chiun said. "A doctor show. Doctor shows are best."

"This is Wesley Pruiss," Smith said.

"Who's he?" asked Remo.

"The publisher of *Gross*."

"Serves him right," Remo said.

Theodosia was on screen now. She wore a white linen pants suit. It was tailored tightly to her body, but the basic business cut of the suit surrendered to the cut of her own full, voluptuous body.

"Too fat," Chiun said. "The women are always too fat on these shows."

Theodosia spoke.

"It was only through good fortune that this cowardly attack did not kill Wesley. To make sure that no such attack will ever again have any chance of success, I plan to spend every penny, if necessary, of Wesley's fortune to hire the best bodyguards in the world to protect him."

An off-camera voice drawled: "Why?"

Theodosia wheeled. Her eyes glared at the off-camera voice.

"I'll tell you why," she said. "Because I love him. Because he is going to make his mark in this world. Because what he's doing out here may be the most important thing done in this country since Kitty Hawk. That's why. That's why I'm going to make sure he lives. Does that answer your question?"

The camera slid back and showed Theodosia stand-

45

ing in front of a big building that looked like a pre-Civil War mansion, talking to a cluster of reporters.

"And that's the way it is here in Furlong County," an announcer's voice said. Then the tape ended and the screen went dark.

"So what?" Remo said.

"That's all there is?" Chiun asked. "A fat man in bed and a fat woman complaining about everything? What kind of story is that?"

"That was on tonight's news," Smith told Remo.

"I don't watch the news," Chiun said.

"Again, so what?" Remo asked.

"I want you to get the job as his bodyguard," Smith said.

"What the hell for?"

"Because when Pruiss moved out to that county in Indiana, he said he was going to make the entire county an experimental showcase for solar energy. He has to be kept alive to make sure that project goes ahead."

"Let the government do it," Remo said. "Why him?"

"Because you know as well as I do that the government can't do it," Smith said. "They'll take ten years passing legislation, ten years writing regulations, ten years bringing polluters to court, and at the end of it, we still won't have a solar energy program and we'll be burning blubber in lamps to try to keep warm."

Remo thought about that for a moment, then nodded.

Chiun said, "Blubber has a funny smell."

"Who tried to kill him?" Remo asked Smith.

"We don't know," Smith said. "Somebody with a knife. God knows he's got enough enemies. But we don't want him killed. Keeping him alive is your job."

46

Chiun waited until the door was closed behind Smith and said, "That was a stupid show."

"It wasn't a show, Chiun. It's our next job: Keeping Wesley Pruiss alive."

"Who is this Wesley Pruiss?"

"He publishes magazines," Remo said.

"Good."

"Why good?" Remo asked.

"Because now maybe my novels and stories will get published and I can finally overcome this anti-Korean prejudice against great art."

"Your novels and stories won't get published until you write them," Remo said.

"You are not going to discourage me," Chiun said. "All I have to do is put them down on paper. They are all up here." He tapped a forefinger to his temple. "Every beautiful word, every exquisite scene, every brilliant insight. All up here. All I have to do is put them onto paper and that is the easiest part. What is the name of this magazine?"

"*Gross*," Remo said.

"Yes," Chiun said. "What is the name of this magazine?"

"Its name is *Gross*," Remo said.

"Hmmmm," said Chiun. "I didn't know you had a magazine named after you."

The Reverend Higbe Muckley could not read or write, but since that had never been a barrier to getting on network television, he had manipulated television very well to become a millionaire several times over. He had always been able to count very well.

The Reverend Mr. Muckley had hit upon the simple trick of selling memberships in his Divine Right church; five dollars to be a deacon, ten dollars to be a minister, fifteen dollars for an auxiliary bishop, one hundred dollars for a full bishopric, along with a life-long free subscription to Muckley's magazine, *Divine Right*, an almost incomprehensible word-by-word transcription of Muckley's confused ramblings, printed six times a year, more or less, depending on how long it took the copies of the last issue to vanish. Any full-fledged official in the Divine Right church was entitled to men-of-the-cloth discounts in most stores and businesses, and buying a new car at 650 dollars less than the normal going price more than justified the one-time donation to Muckley's church.

Muckley was in his office in the basement of a massage parlor on Ventura Boulevard in West Hollywood when his secretary came into his office. She was not able to read or write very well either, but had achieved professional success in life pretty much by being able to jot down 38-22-36 on application forms.

"Wesley Pruiss has been stabbed," she said. "Almost killed."

"Yes," Muckley said noncommitally.

"I thought you should know," she said. "Maybe it would be something for you to do something with."

"Yes," he said again.

His secretary realized he must be thinking of money when he did not try to grab her in his office. After she left, Muckley continued thinking. New memberships were down because he had not been featured on any network news in almost three months. And he smiled, because God always showed the way. He had delivered Wesley Pruiss into Higbe Muckley's hands.

He called a "must" prayer meeting for the follow-

48

ing day of all his West Coast disciples, or as many could borrow the bus fare to Hollywood.

At Muckley's invitation, all the networks showed up. Reporters liked to cover Higbe Muckley. He was an easy story, and in contrast with his backwoods drawl, they always managed to look smart.

Muckley led his disciples in a prayer that thanked God for goodness, right, money, biodegradable soap and instant mashed potatoes, as long as they were made without any of them godless chemicals.

Then he had special thanks for God.

"In his charity and mercy and wisdom, God has seen fit to strike down a purveyor of dirt and filth who is trying to carry his disgusting New York City message to the heartland of America," Muckley said. He looked around at the audience.

"Can we let this man do that?"

"No," came back two hundred voices, sounding like five thousand and looking like five hundred in the too-small meeting room Muckley had rented.

"That's right," Muckley said. "Get this down, you gentlemen of the press. Tonight I'm going to Furlong County, Indiana, and I'm going to lead a prayer vigil there for all the faithful to make sure that this West-burg Purse . . ." he paused as his secretary whispered in his ear, ". . . to make sure that this Westerly Prunes abandons his sinful life."

Later Muckley was asked what if Wesley Pruiss did not abandon his sinful life.

Muckley was thoughtful for a moment. He had learned through experience that pregnant pauses always looked good during television interviews. "Well," he said finally, "in that case we have to remember what God said."

"What did God say?"

49

"He said that here on earth, God's work has to be done by men."

The sign on the door read "For Useful Effective Leadership." Under it a larger sign warned: "Keep out."

Inside the large room, twelve men sat on straight-backed chairs. They wore metal caps with sensor devices built into them, and attached by wires to panels at the right side of their chairs.

The twelve men were looking at a motion picture screen, still blank at the front of the brightly-lit room.

Behind the men, Will Bobbin, assistant director of community relations for the National Fossil Fuel Institute, nervously twisted a strand of his thinning gray hair, then flicked off the room lights and turned on the movie projector. Its fan began to whir and then the lamp lit and a picture appeared on the movie screen.

It was a picture of a small room, bare of furniture except for two wooden chairs. A door at the side of the room opened and a tall, elderly man wearing just a white shirt and trousers came in. Behind him came a gray-haired woman. She was blind and carried a white cane and wore heavy smoked glasses. Her bluish gray hair was immaculately marcelled and as the man took her arm to help her into her chair, she smiled a smile of pure warmth and love. She looked like everyone's storybook grandmother.

Bobbin glanced around the room. The twelve men were staring frontwards at the old couple on the movie screen. The men did not know it, but they were about to take part in a test that would determine forever their future in the coal and oil industry. Will Bobbin had designed the test.

The old couple sat on the chairs on screen, smiling straight ahead at the camera. The camera must have been hidden because the smiles were unselfconscious.

Bobbin waved to a team of three men he knew were hidden behind a large glass mirror on the right of the room. The signal was to make sure all the sensor-recording devices were on, to measure the emotional reactions of the twelve men to what they were about to see.

After a few seconds, the old couple stopped smiling. The man put his arms around the woman's shoulders and pulled her toward him, as if to share their body warmth. The woman said something to him and, as she spoke, breath steamed in front of her face.

The temperature in the room pictured on the screen was clearly going lower. With his free hand, the man turned up his shirt collar and buttoned it up at the neck. He hunched his shoulders, as people do in the cold, to try to pocket their bodily heat.

The couple talked to each other again but the film was silent and the men in the room could not hear voices. The woman wept. Tears rolled down her pink round cheeks. The camera zoomed in for a closeup and the tears turned to ice drops halfway down the woman's face.

The tall old man got up and walked to the door through which they had entered. He tried the knob. It would not turn. He yanked at the door. The blind woman still sat on the chair, but turned her head from side to side in confusion. The old man pounded on the door, but there was obviously no reply, because his face grew sad, and he came back and sat down again next to the old woman and tried to comfort her.

51

The film went on. The steam from their breaths frosted into ice in their hair and eyebrows. They hugged each other tightly, but when that failed to keep them warm, the man took off his shirt and put it around the woman. Then he kissed her on the mouth, and they clung to each other, tightly locked in each others arms.

The film seemed to skip for a moment, and then the couple was on screen again. They were in the same position, smiles on their faces, but they were coated with ice and obviously frozen to death. Bobbin heard someone gag in the front of the room. The film skipped again and showed the two people frozen in place, each coated with an inch-thick slick of ice.

It skipped again. Bobbin heard someone start to throw up. The final frames of the film showed the people now covered in a mound of ice, the ice so thick that one had to look hard to discern under the block the forms of two real people.

Bobbin froze the final frame of the movie and flicked on the lights. He walked to the front of the room and looked around. One man had thrown up onto the floor. Another had his handkerchief to his mouth and was gagging into it. They were out of it. They would never move up in the fuel industry. Some of the men seemed shocked. They were losers too.

Three men looked up at Bobbin with questioning eyes that showed no emotional reaction at all. They would probably reach the second level of management.

But two men looked at Bobbin very differently. Their eyes glistened with a vision of positive enjoyment. There were smiles on their faces. These two were comers, Bobbin knew. Some day they would head oil companies or coal companies.

Bobbin spoke. "You just saw a film. That's all, a film."

The man who had thrown up kept retching on the floor. The others watched Bobbin.

"That's all," he repeated. "A film. It's not like we go around freezing people all the time. We didn't even freeze these people at all."

Some of the men looked relieved at hearing it was a bloodless experiment. Bobbin paused to make sure that the sensors recorded their reaction to his remark. The two men who had seemed to enjoy the film looked disappointed at what Bobbin said. But they smiled again when he added:

"No, we didn't freeze them at all. Somebody else froze them." The sick man threw up some more.

"We just photographed them," Bobbin said. "That's all. The freezing wasn't our responsibility. As a matter of fact, and your news networks never mention a thing like this, you never hear that they owed money for fuel bills, the blind lady never paid a fuel bill in her whole fucking life. But the news never mentions that. No. Old people dying is always dramatic so it gets on the news. But it's not the whole story, not by a long shot."

Bobbin stopped. That was certainly enough for the people operating the sensor recorders to give him full reports on the leadership potential of the twelve men, all mid-level executives in the fossil fuel industry.

Bobbin felt good. He would bet that this screening system was going to work and if it did, his reputation was made. It was costly and dangerous for the fuel industry to go grooming top-level executives and then, when they got into the top slots, to find out that they had social consciences and a sense of the responsibility of the fuel companies to the public, and all those other things that were good for political speeches, but played hob with the oil and coal companies' profit and loss statements. Not to mention annual dividends.

"We want to thank all you gentlemen for coming to New York," Bobbin said. "Of course, you realize that this experimental program is being kept absolutely quiet so you will not talk about it. Now lunch is being served in the presidential dining room." He smiled. His fingers strayed toward the wisp of gray hair in front of his right ear.

"Good lunch, too," he said. "Salad with Roquefort dressing, vichyssoise, broiled lobster—fresh lobster, too, none of that frozen stuff. I guess you've had enough frozen meat for one day. Enjoy, enjoy."

The sick man heaved up some more. A loser, Bobbin thought. Just a loser.

After the room had been cleared, Bobbin waved toward the one-way window and a technician in a white smock entered the room.

"Got everything?" Bobbin asked.

"Got it all."

"On my desk when?"

"Tomorrow."

"Fine," Bobbin said.

The man in the white jacket left. Bobbin's assistant ran into the room.

"Bad news, Will," he said.

"What's that?" Bobbin asked, annoyed that he should have to listen to somebody's idea of bad news on a day that had thus far gone so well.

"Wesley Pruiss is still alive."

"Shit," said Bobbin.

"What'll we do? If he goes ahead with that solar energy project . . ." The assistant did not finish the sentence but his tone of impending doom finished it for him.

"Leave it to me," Bobbin said with a grim smile. "Leave it to me." And he started twisting the hair at his right temple again.

CHAPTER FOUR

Theodosia had taken over the entire east wing of the Furlong General Hospital and turned it into a fortress for Wesley Pruiss.

Contractors had been hurriedly hired to seal off all the connections between the main hospital and the new east wing. Meanwhile other contractors were bolting solid steel plates over the doors and windows.

When the job was done, there was only one way to enter the east wing. From the downstairs ground level entrance door, which was locked and guarded twentyfour hours a day by one of the Furlong County police, there was no way to get out of the stairwell before the top floor where Wesley Pruiss lay in a bed in the only room in the wing that was occupied.

Inside the stairwell, outside the top floor, stood a mercenary colonel who had grown famous for his exploits leading men in African wars. He carried a small submachine gun and an auto-Mag pistol.

He had been the first of three bodyguards hired by Theodosia.

Behind the door the colonel guarded and patrolling the ten feet of distance from the hall door to Pruiss's room was a man who had been the world's middleweight karate champion. He could drive his foot through a plaster wall. His hands were gnarled and hard enough to drive nails. He was the second bodyguard.

The third was a former Olympic champion in small arms fire, a consultant in weaponry to the Los Angeles and New York police departments.

All the windows of Wesley Pruiss's room had been blocked off with steel plates, except for one that caught the morning sun. The window opened onto a fire escape and through it Pruiss was able to see the country club building that had been his home and the Furlong County golf course. On the fire escape of Pruiss's room, the small arms expert watched the roof above, the ground below and the metal steps leading up the fire escape. He carried a .357 Magnum and a .22 caliber semi-automatic pistol.

As an extra precaution, the window behind him had been wired to administer a killing shock to anyone who tried to open it without the power being turned off from inside the room.

Each man was being paid two thousand dollars a week. Theodosia felt secure. No one was just going to walk into Wesley Pruiss's room and harm him. Not with these security precautions.

She stopped outside the clubhouse that was now the Pruiss mansion and picked some pink and red flowers. Her chauffeur let her off at the one working door to the hospital's east wing.

The policeman at the door recognized her, but according to instructions, he stayed behind the locked door until she repeated the password: *"Gross* is beautiful."

Only then did he let her into the downstairs hallway, quickly closing the door behind her. He checked her purse for weapons and then inspected the bunch of flowers. Only when he was satisfied that everything was in order, did he say, "Morning, Miss Theodosia."

"Morning. Everything quiet?"

"Yes, Ma'am."

She walked up the three double flights of stairs to the fourth floor. As she turned the corner of the steps near the top, she saw the mercenary colonel, wearing khaki battle gear, pointing a submachine gun at her.

"Morning, mum," he said in a crisp British accent.

He too checked her purse and flowers, then turned and knocked four times on the door leading to the corridor.

Theodosia smiled as she watched her professionals go through their professional extra-safe procedures.

She heard the door unlock from the inside. The colonel counted to six before opening it.

"If it opens right away," he explained to her, "the man inside will attack."

He pulled the door open and Theodosia went inside. The karate expert, wearing a loose-fitting gi and barefooted, was in an attack stance that relaxed only when he recognized Theodosia.

He too checked purse and flowers.

She smiled again. She pushed through the swinging door into Wesley Pruiss's room. The small arms expert was on the fire escape, looking down and up and around in a never-ending cycle of vigilance.

Wesley Pruiss was still asleep when she entered the room and Theodosia smiled when she saw the gentle, almost boyish look on his placid face. And then her eyes widened in shock.

There was a yellow tag on the front of Pruiss's pajamas. It had writing on it. She moved quickly to the side of his bed and looked down at the tag. It was the inside of a matchbook from which the striker had been torn. The note had been written with a black felt-tipped marker that lay alongside Pruiss's bed with his notepad.

The note read: "Your bodyguards stink." And there was a telephone number after it.

The note had been clipped to the lapel of Pruiss's pajamas with a safety pin and when she removed it, Pruiss woke up and saw her.

She pushed the yellow cardboard into her purse.

"Morning, love," Pruiss said.

She bent over to kiss him, then handed him the flowers. Without even a glance, he dropped them on the table next to his bed.

"I'm sorry I woke you up," she said.

"All right," he said. His voice was deep with despondency. "What else have I got to do but sleep?"

"Don't say that, Wesley. You're going to be as good as new."

"Yeah. As good as a new cripple can be," he said bitterly.

He turned away. When he looked back, he saw her still smiling at him, very bravely. As a reward, he smiled himself.

"Did you sleep well?" she asked.

"Why not? With all those guards you've got around here, who could wake me up?"

"No one came in to bother you?"

"No," Pruiss said. "I just wish somebody had. I wish

60

that guy with the knife had come back and finished the job."

"I won't hear that, Wesley," said Theodosia, her face flushed with anger. "You're an important man. You're going to be even more important. The world can't afford the loss of a man like you."

"It's lost half of me already. The leg half. Don't kid me, Theodosia. I know hopeless when I see hopeless. So do the doctors. Spinal injury. Cripple."

"What do those doctors know?" she asked. "We'll get more doctors. Better doctors."

He thought about that for a moment, looking out the window at the bright sky.

"Maybe, you're right," he said. "You know, there are times when I feel that there's some life in my legs . . . like I could almost move them. Not much and not often. But once in a while."

He looked at Theodosia for some expression. He caught a brief flash of sorrow on her face that she turned into a smile as she said, "See. You never can tell." But her face told him a different story. It was hopeless and she knew it. He was a cripple, doomed to be a cripple for the rest of his life.

He closed his eyes and said nothing more. He opened his mouth to take the pain pills she gave him and he had nothing to say when she began arranging for an ambulance to take him from the hospital back to the country club where his master bedroom had been converted into a hospital room. But it felt good, even if he wouldn't admit it to her, to be out of the hospital and back to his home, even if it was a new home and one he had not yet had a chance to get used to.

When she went out in the early afternoon, Theodosia left the three bodyguards in his bedroom with orders to leave under no circumstances.

Before leaving the building, she fished the piece of yellow cardboard from her purse and telephoned the number on it.

Remo was lying on the bed in Room 15 of the Furlong Budget Value Dollar Motel when Theodosia rapped firmly on the door.

When he opened it he looked her up and down and asked, "Who are you? Not that it really matters all that much."

"You're the one who left the note?" Theodosia asked.

"Right. That's right," Remo said. "I saw you on television. Ambrosia or something."

"Theodosia."

"Come on in."

He went back to the bed while Theodosia sat on the couch.

"How did you get into that hospital room?" asked Theodosia.

"Don't answer that, Remo," Chiun said as he appeared in the doorway connecting Room 15 and his own Room 17.

"Why not?" Remo asked.

"Because she has not paid you anything and even if she had, we do not give our secrets away. We sell our performance but not knowledge of our techniques."

"Very wise," Theodosia said.

"Actually, it just sounds wise," Remo said. "Even if I told, you wouldn't understand the techniques."

"Try me," said Theodosia. There was a small smile on her face, the smile of a woman who had been underestimated many times before by men who thought that because she had enough chest for everybody, it automatically followed that she didn't have a brain in her head.

"All right," Remo said, holding back a smile of his own. "We saw the guard on the fire escape, the one in the stairwell, the one outside the door. Plus the slug guarding the front door. We only wanted to go into the room, not hurt anybody. So we didn't go any of those ways."

"So mystically we appeared, masked in the cloak of ,invisibility," said Chiun, with a warning glance at Remo.

Theodosia smiled at him. Chiun smiled back.

Remo shook his head. "No. We figured you had all the openings to the room covered but you didn't cover the non-openings, so we turned a non-opening into an opening."

He nodded to her.

"The windows," she said. "You got in through a window."

"You'll never know that," Remo said. "Now *that's* a secret."

"But how did you get to a window? The roof is sealed off and there's only one fire escape up the side, and that one's guarded."

"Secret," Remo said.

"Yes," said Chiun. "Remo is right. It is very secret. We would like to tell you, young lady, but if we tell you, you will tell someone else and he will tell someone else and before you know it, everyone will know how to climb the sides of smooth walls and remove steel plates from over windows and then replace the plates on the way back down. So we cannot tell you."

"Thank you, Little Father," Remo said, "for not telling."

Chiun nodded his appreciation.

"How much?" Theodosia said.

"What are you paying those three blocks you've got now? I guess the cop on the front door is free."

Theodosia nodded. Chiun cleared his throat.

"A thousand a week each," Theodosia said.

"That means two thousand a week," Remo said.

Chiun cleared his throat again. Remo ignored him.

"That's a total of six thousand a week," Remo said. "Since we're incalculably better than they are, we can't apply a percentage to it. But let's say, ten thousand a week."

"Too much," Theodosia said.

Chiun cleared his throat again and Remo looked at him in annoyance, before glancing back at the woman.

"Suit yourself," Remo said. "We can always go to work for the people who want to get rid of him."

"You know who they are?" the woman said warily. She had a pencil in her hand but she jabbed it angrily against her small note pad as she asked the question.

"No, but it shouldn't be hard to find them if we'd a mind to," Remo said. Chiun cleared his throat again.

"You think so?" said Theodosia.

"I know so," said Chiun, before Remo could answer. The old Oriental looked confidently at the young dark-haired woman.

"All right. Ten thousand a week. Guard Wesley and find out who's responsible for that attack on him."

Chiun raised a finger. "Not quite," he said, "Who pays for these hotel rooms?"

Theodosia looked around at the worn bedspread, the walked-thin carpet, the water-stained wallpaper near the door.

"All right," she said. "I'll throw in the rooms too."

"Fine," said Chiun. He looked triumphantly at Remo, then leaned closer to him. "See," he said in Korean. "how easily it all goes if you leave the negotiating to me."

In his halting Korean, Remo said, "Chiun, I would have gotten the same money. All you did was get us another job, finding out who hit Pruiss."

"I got us the hotel rooms paid for," Chiun said. His voice raised as he became excited.

"The rooms only cost us six dollars, for Chrissakes," Remo said. "You gave away an extra job for six dollars. No wonder Sinanju's a poor village."

"You speak terrible Korean," Chiun said. "I can't understand a word you say."

"I said I would have gotten the same money."

"You wouldn't have," Chiun insisted. "Negotiating is one of the special skills of Masters of Sinanju."

"Would," said Remo in English.

"Wouldn't," said Chiun.

Theodosia stood up.

"Why not come with me now?" she said.

Remo started off the bed.

"Not so fast," Chiun said.

"What now?" asked Remo.

"The hotel room keys," he said. "Give them to her." He pointed to Theodosia as if he expected her to run out of the room. She smiled at Remo who shrugged.

"Anything you say, Chiun. Anything you say," said Remo wearily.

Wesley Pruiss was drinking beer from a can when they arrived back at the country club. Theodosia sent the three bodyguards outside, then snatched the can of Rheingold Extra Light away from Pruiss.

"Hey," he said.

"Hey yourself," she said. "No drinking. You know that."

"What difference does it make?"

He saw Remo and Chiun standing at the foot of his bed. He had not heard them enter the room.

"Who are these guys?"

"Your new bodyguards."

Pruiss looked at them carefully, his face seemingly undecided between a scowl and a sneer. "Body-guards. They look just about right to guard half a man."

"You were a half a man before you got hurt, Pruiss," Remo said.

"Is that how you talk to all your employers? What are we paying these guys?" he asked Theodosia.

"Remo, leave this to me," hissed Chiun. "Not nearly as much as we usually charge for such services," he told Pruiss quickly. "But we came along just for the pleasure of protecting such an enlightened person as you." He smiled and folded his hands inside the sleeves of his flowing green evening robe.

"You did, huh?" Pruiss's voice was still wary but his face showed satisfaction at the ego-stroking.

"Yes," said Chiun. "Would you like to hear my poetry?"

"No," said Pruiss.

"Some other time," Chiun said agreeably.

"I doubt it," Pruiss said.

"Don't doubt it," Remo said. "You're going to hear so much Ung poetry that you're going to be able to recite it, Pruiss. You'll learn it by heart. In Korean. You'll be able to give us three hours on a flower open-ing and two more hours on a bee landing on the flower. You'll be the life of the orgy."

"Don't give away the story," Chiun told Remo.

"Get these two out of here," Pruiss told Theodosia.

"Suits me," Remo said. "The only reason we'd even take this job is so you can go ahead and do your thing with solar energy. Sure as hell not because we like you."

Pruiss waved his hand, dismissing solar energy.

Remo waved his hand back.

"The hell with solar energy," Pruiss said. "I don't care if everybody freezes to death."

Theodosia stood alongside Pruiss, looking at Remo and Chiun. She said blandly, "I don't think Wesley really feels that way. It's just the strain of everything."

"Strain, my butt. That's the way I really feel," Pruiss said.

"Swell," said Remo. "Come on, Chiun, let's go."

After they had passed the guards in the hallway, Chiun asked Remo: "Why did you say that?"

"She pulls the strings," Remo said. "Let her work on him. It's better than us arguing with him."

They walked down the broad curved staircase of the old country club and out the front door into the pleasant spring night of Indiana.

At the end of the long driveway was a small street. Across the street stood the reconstructed tenement building.

"That is where it happened?" Chiun asked.

"Yes."

"I would see it."

The moonlight streamed in through the kitchen window and illuminated the kerosene lamp on the table. Remo went to light it with a match, while Chiun went unerringly toward the other end of the railroad apartment. When Remo had the light on, he turned to see Chiun crouched down, feeling the floor.

"This is where the assassin stood," Chiun said.

"How can you tell that?"

"Because he was here waiting for Pruiss. This is the only spot in this room where the floorboards do not creak. He could have stood here in perfect silence to wait his moment."

Remo nodded.

"A knife thrown from the blackness of night," Chiun said softly, more to himself than to Remo. "This is not good."

"Why?" Remo asked.

Chiun seemed to ignore the question as he rose and stared at the floor. "The man stood here," he said, "and waited for the big-mouthed one to enter the room. Then, across a distance of twenty feet, he threw a knife that almost took the life from Pruiss. But not quite. Now, he was alone with his victim. Did he then go to him to finish his task? No."

"Maybe something scared him off," Remo said?

"No," said Chiun.

"Why not?"

"He had time to go to his victim and remove the knife. All he had to do was to twist it and his victim would be dead and his mission accomplished. But he did not do that. He just removed the knife and fled. Why?"

Remo shrugged.

"Really, Remo. Sometimes you are very dense."

"I'm glad now it's only sometimes. Usually you tell me I'm always very dense."

"Have it your own way," Chiun said. "Remo, you are always very dense and never more so than now."

"All right. You tell me."

"Yes," said Chiun. "I do not think he meant to kill

68

Wesley Pruiss, because otherwise he would have. And I think he had a reason for taking his knife."

"Not to leave fingerprints behind," Remo said.

"He could have just wiped the handle," said Chiun. "He took the knife so we would not see it. Why?"

"Who cares?"

"You should. He took it because it probably identifies him."

"Probably had one of those little tags printed on the handle: 'If found, drop in nearest mailbox. Norman Knifethrower will guarantee postage.'"

Chiun ignored him. He stood up straight and took a pose, left foot in front of his right, almost as if he were fencing an imaginary opponent. He rocked back and forth, transferring his weight from foot to foot. There was only silence in the flat as Remo watched.

"Remo," Chiun said. "Stand here."

He stepped aside as Remo walked over and stood.

"Now, rock from side to side."

Remo did as ordered. The floorboards squeaked beneath his feet.

Chiun sighed. "I have seen enough," he said. "It is time for us to leave."

"So who killed cock robin?" Remo asked.

"I will explain it all to you when you are capable of absorbing what I tell you. But let me warn you. We are facing a very dangerous man, very formidable. His skill is not greatly different from ours."

"You can tell all that by listening to the floor boards not squeak?"

"Everything hands over its secrets to one who demands them," Chiun said. "I can tell you something more too," he added as he started for the kitchen door. Remo blew out the kerosene lamp and followed him.

"Yeah? What's that?" Remo asked.

"The assassin will wear a thick black leather belt. The back of the belt will be filled with knives, knives with red leather handles. And near the bloodguard of each knife will be imprinted the outline of a rearing stallion."

And then he was walking down the stairs, shaking his head slowly from side to side. But when Remo caught up to him, Chiun would say no more. He said he wished to think.

There were two calls at the motel that night for Remo.

The first was Smith, who was dismayed when Remo told him that Wesley Pruiss was talking about dropping the solar energy project.

"We can't let that happen," Smith said dourly.

"It won't," Remo said. "Ruby back yet?"

"Not for another week."

"Tell her I got a new job for her if she wants it," Remo said.

"What is that?" Smith asked suspiciously.

"I know a guy. I can get her in as a Grossie Girl."

The second telephone call came from Theodosia.

"You know," she told Remo, "you're not as dumb as you look."

"I know," said Remo. "It's one of my crosses in life, people thinking I'm just another pretty face."

"Anyway, I'm working on Wesley. I'll get him to change his mind on the solar power."

"I know you will," Remo said. "When?"

"Can you start in the morning?" she asked.

"Be there," Remo promised.

The early morning sun turned Furlong County into

a picture postcard. It shone gold off the roofs of the small, neat buildings and almost whitened the fields of early wheat. The small fishing lakes glinted metallically, looking like pits of piled up diamonds. As the sun came over the trees, it sparkled off the dew the night had deposited on the practice putting green in front of the Furlong Country Club.

Pruiss was in the middle of the green, lying in a hospital bed. The imprints of its wheels had pressed deep into the tightly packed grass of the green.

The three bodyguards stood at three different points around the green, facing away from Pruiss. The mercenary colonel and small arms expert were carrying their favorite weapons. The karate man was carrying sirakens, the pointed silver throwing stars, and prowled nervously back and forth over about three feet of the green's perimeter.

Theodosia stood alongside Pruiss's bed, next to a dark-skinned man wearing a jeweled Nehru jacket and a turban with a red stone in the front of it.

As Remo and Chiun approached, the man grabbed the bottom of Pruiss's bed and rolled it around so that the rapidly-rising sun shone directly in Pruiss's eyes.

The mercenary colonel did not notice Remo and Chiun until they were standing next to him. His hand moved to the trigger guard on his gun.

"Easy," Remo said, "we're on the same team."

"Miss Theodosia," the man called in his brisk accent. She looked up and saw Remo and Chiun.

"It's all right, Colonel," she said.

The colonel relaxed his finger grip, but still looked suspiciously at Remo and Chiun. People who came upon him that silently could be up to no good.

"Who's the twerp?" Remo asked him.

"Don't know," the colonel said. "Some bleedin' Indian mystic, I hear."

Wesley Pruiss had the same question.

"Theodosia, who the hell is this?"

The little Indian spoke.

"Rachmed Baya Bam, at your service, sirrrr."

Pruiss ignored him.

"Theo, who is he?"

"He's the head of the Inner Light Movement," she said.

"I gave at the office," Pruiss said.

"Very funny," Rachmed Baya Bam said in his clipped, high pitched voice. "The sahib has a very keen sense of the humorous. So do I, Rachmed Baya Bam, chosen by the Almighty to be the head of the Inner Light Movement. I am the man who harnesses the strength of the sun, the peace force of the universe, the creator of all that is good and strong. That is what I do, sirrr," he told Pruiss. He hissd his s's as he spoke.

"Rachmed has come to help," Theodosia said.

"Yeah," Pruiss said in disgust. "To help himself."

"Wesley, give him a chance," Theodosia said. "Can it hurt?"

Baya Bam paid no attention to her. He slowly lifted the covers on the bottom of Pruiss's bed, exposing the publisher's pale, thin legs to the sunlight.

He stood alongside the foot of the bed and turned his face to the sun. He raised his hands above his head and began to chant. There were occasional words in English but most of the words Remo could not understand.

"What's he saying, Chiun?" asked Remo.

"He is saying nonsense," Chiun said.

Baya Bam switched to English.

72

"Oh, almighty power of the golden orb, bring the strengthness and goodness of your peace force into these legs. Bring life where there is no life. Bring strength where there is only weakness."

Pruiss turned his face away from Baya Bam. The look on his face would have been appropriate if he had seen the man eating spiders.

Baya Bam laid hands on Pruiss's legs. He kneaded the muscles, then reached his hands above his head again toward the sun, as if refilling their supply of strength, and then reached down quickly, gripping Pruiss's calf muscles and squeezing hard.

Pruiss winced.

"Ouch," he said.

Theodosia squealed and threw her arms around his shoulders and kissed his face.

"Wesley, you felt it. You felt it," she said excitedly.

"Huh?" said Pruiss.

"Don't you see?" she said. "You felt his pressure on your legs. They're not dead anymore."

Pruiss looked stupid for a moment, then smiled and turned toward Rachmed Baya Bam. But the small Indian had turned his back to Pruiss and was again looking at the sun, now well above the string of trees bordering the first fairway of the golf course.

"Oh, holy globe," Baya Bam said. "We thank you in the glory of your power and in showing us the way of the inner light. And we thank you for opening the eyes of this unbeliever to show him that all things wait for him who leads the good life and who glorifies your power and virtue. All hail, oh, golden one."

He turned back and told Theodosia. "That is enough for now. We can do no more today."

"I felt it," Pruiss said. "I felt it. He squeezed my legs and I felt it." He looked around to the body-

73

guards to share his good news with them, but, professionally, they had their backs turned to him. He saw Remo and Chiun and greeted them with a smile.

"I felt it," he said.

"Yes, Wesley," Theodosia said. "We know."

She called to the three bodyguards. "All right, let's get Mr. Pruiss inside before he catches a chill." She pulled the bed's covers down over his legs. The three guards came and began rolling the bed away.

She followed them but stopped to say to Remo, "I have to give Wesley the pain pills for his legs."

Rachmed Baya Bam still stood facing the sun in the center of the putting green. Remo decided that if you put knickers and a turban on a gorilla, there would still be no trouble finding some people to call it a holy man.

"Do you want to talk to him, Chiun?" asked Remo.

"No," said Chiun.

They went into the big building. They heard Rachmed Baya Bam following them, almost running to keep up.

They all walked past the three bodyguards, who stood in the hallway outside Pruiss's room, and went inside. The publisher's face broke into a smile when he saw the Indian. He nodded coolly toward Remo and Chiun. "I guess you two can stay too," he said.

Baya Bam stood at the side of Pruiss's bed.

"Guru," Pruiss said. "I want to thank you. You've given me my first taste of hope."

"Sirrr," Baya Bam said. "It has nothing to do with me. I am merely the vessel through which the sun's power is poured."

"A fraud," Chiun told Remo. "Next he'll be saying that he's the sun source."

74

"The sun is the source and I am merely the conduit through which it flows," the Indian said.

"See," said Remo. "At least he's more modest than you."

"He should be," Chiun said.

"Anything I can have, guru, you can have," Pruiss said.

Baya Bam smiled, a smile Remo recognized as that of a man who had wired aces in a game of stud poker.

"The sun will make you whole," Baya Bam said, "because the sun can do all things. So should you not share that goodness with all people?"

Pruiss looked dumb for a moment, then asked, "Solar energy?"

"Yesss," said the Indian. "The sun can cure you and it will do that to make you ready for your mission in life. To bring the sun and its power to all the people of the world for their betterment."

"That's all you want?" Pruiss asked.

"Yes," Baya Bam said. "That is all." He paused. "That is a very handsome wristwatch you wear, sirrrr."

Pruiss stripped it from his wrist and it vanished from his fingertips into the folds of Baya Bam's pantaloons before the publisher could change his mind. Theodosia looked pained.

"You really think there's hope?" said Pruiss.

"There is more than hope. A cure is a certainty," the Indian said.

"Touch my legs again?"

The Indian shook his head. "Not today. Enough for today. Even the sun needs time to grow the tree."

"That's a good one, Chiun," said Remo. "Why don't you write it down so you can use it sometime?"

Chiun looked at Remo coldly. Pruiss was nodding at Baya Bam.

"I'll do it," he said. "Theo, the solar project's back on. And if I get cured . . ."

"When," corrected Baya Bam.

"When I'm cured, I'm offering my life up to the sun. Maybe make movies about it. Work it into the pictures. *Sunny Sexcapades*. No. I'll think about it. Maybe even give up the porn. Change the Gross-Outs into Sun-Spots. Serve health food. Guava jelly and some kind of crackers. No more frozen mayonaisse. Make 'em family places. Bring the kids and all." His face looked dreamy as his voice slowly trailed off and Wesley Pruiss fell asleep on his pillow.

"Guru," said Theodosia, "you are welcome to stay here for as long as you wish."

"Thank you, little lady," said Baya Bam.

"He is a fraud," Chiun told Remo.

CHAPTER FIVE

Security meant not being afraid when you were summoned to the boss's office. This thought came to Will Bobbin as he walked, whistling, down the hall to the office of the director of community relations for the National Fossil Fuels Institute. He was no longer afraid: he was secure in his job.

And it had taken him a long time to achieve that goal.

When he had first come to work for the institute, he had anticipated making the oil and coal industries forward-looking, responsive to the public good. In his occasional appearances on television talk shows, he was always cool and articulate, nodding gently and concernedly when anti-oil bigots attacked the major producers, quietly awaiting his chance to systematically demolish them with impeccable logic. He fancied them as Tchaikovskian bursts of noise and himself as the gentle, precise melody of "Liebestraum."

He had been sure his performance was being noticed upstairs. And whenever one of the presidents of an oil company had died, he had harbored the small hope—one he was unwilling to admit even to himself—that someone in the industry with foresight and imagination would recognize his merit and reach down into the ranks and snatch him up for president. And then he could show them how to run an oil company. How to make profits and still be sensitive to the public's wishes. How to balance the bottom line for the company—profits—with the bottom line for humanity, which was "concern for the well-being of our country . . . nay, even for our species," as he had once said on an interview show.

But no one had reached down to anoint him as a president, and as time went on, it slowly began to sink in that no one in the business took him seriously. His boss was fond of saying to him, while reading a report and talking on the telephone at the same time, "Yes, yes, Bobbin, that's very interesting, send me a memo if you get a chance."

One day, after he had been with the institute for more than ten years, he took a look around and realized that everyone who had joined the company at about the same time he had, had already been promoted upstairs while he was still in the same dead-ended job.

He thought about it for a long while and decided that the difference between them and him was that they were jingoistic fools who believed in the fossil fuels industry, right or wrong, and they would never attain his special higher form of intellectual grace. On the other hand, they were all making over fifty thousand dollars a year, and still climbing.

So Bobbin looked carefully at the industry that had obviously spurned his enlightened ideas, and he looked at the mortgage on his house and the college bills for his kids and the amount he still owed on his summer home, and he came to the decision that the fuel industry would have rewarded his genius if they had been allowed to. But they had been prevented from doing that by an avaricious American public that always wanted something for nothing and by a greedy, grasping government that wanted to steal all your profits in tax dollars so they could piss them away on the unworthy.

This Jesuitical judgment allowed Bobbin to hate the American consumer and the American government instead of the industry that had rejected him. And he hated with a passion. His voice became one of the most strident in the industry, attacking the looneys and the fuzzy-brains and the free-lunch grubbers.

Gone was the thoughtful, professorial Will Bobbin of the early days. Gone were the gentle explanations on talk shows of the oil company position. Instead, Bobbin turned into a gut fighter, always looking for an edge, shouting down opponents with performances that would have sickened him ten years earlier.

And the promotions had followed. And the raises.

Then he had developed his screening program for potential oil executives.

"What's the point of all this?" the head of the lobby had asked him.

Bobbin had laid on him his very best, knowing, sardonic smile.

"Just to prevent the wrong kind of guy from getting to run one of our companies someday," he said.

"Oh? And what is the wrong kind of guy?"

"The kind of guy I used to be," Bobbin said.

The head of the institute had smiled and given him the go-ahead for the program. They had used professional models in the films of the old people freezing, and then used life-sized mannikins underneath the ice for the later shots.

Bobbin supervised the filming himself and kept asking the cameraman and the director for "realism, dammit, more realism. I want to feel those old fucks shiver and twitch. I want to hear their flesh turning hard and their blood congealing. Make it realistic."

For a few moments, Bobbin had thought of finding some old couple who were willing to enter a suicide pact and to lay a lot of money on their estate if they were willing to freeze to death on camera. But he rejected that idea because it might just to be too hard to find such a couple and he wanted to get the film shot and the program in operation as soon as possible. He could be delayed months, just to look for some old gas guzzlers who wanted to die.

The program had gone well and Will Bobbin had promotion on his mind when he walked into his boss's office. But a look at his boss's face had driven that idea from his mind, and for just a moment, he felt the same old twinge of fear he had felt in the early days when he was being called on the carpet.

"Bobbin, you see what this sucker's doing?"

"Which sucker is that?"

"Wesley Pruiss." His boss, a big man with big brutish hands with hair all up and down the backs of his fingers, waved a New York Times at Bobbin, who already had read the story. "He's going ahead with that solar energy shit. You'd think a guy gets crippled, he'd have enough sense to do what he's supposed to do. Go home and play with himself or something."

"I saw the story," Bobbin said. "Bad news."

"Well?"

"Well, what?" Bobbin asked with a small sinking feeling.

"You said you could take care of it."

Bobbin nodded.

"Then you better do it. There's no room in this business, Bobbin, for weaklings who can't see their duty and do it. You get my drift?"

Shaken, Bobbin rose to his feet and nodded. He was dismissed by a curt nod of the head. As he walked from the office, he vowed to himself that he had not come this far in the business just to have his life messed up by some porn publisher. If it turned into a question of the good life for Will Bobbin or life for Wesley Pruiss, well then Wesley Pruiss had just better duck.

The assassin stood in the woods behind the Furlong County Golf Course. He was a small man, dressed casually in khaki slacks and a yellow sports shirt, and he would have looked like many other small men in Furlong County if it had not been for the fact that his skin, like his shirt, was yellow.

His attention was fixed on a squirrel, hopping along a felled tree. The squirrel moved a foot in a nervous hop, stopped, with his plumed tail waving about, then hopped again, all in a quick, herky-jerky movement.

Slowly, the assassin bent down and picked up a small stone in his left hand. He tossed it up into the air, about ten feet high, in the general direction of the squirrel. The stone bounced off the log behind the squirrel who took off as if propelled by a diarrhetic jet.

The animal raced the ten feet down the log, across two feet of open space, hopped onto the trunk of a fat black tree and flashed up toward safety.

The assassin's right hand sped almost like an electric spark toward the back of the thick black leather belt he wore. In one smooth movement, he extracted a red handled knife, brought it up to his ear, and let fly.

The knife made one fast half-turn in the air and then slammed into the squirrel's tail, ripping through the fur and flesh and burying itself an inch deep into the wood of the tree. The squirrel kept trying to climb but, pinned by the knife, was unable to move and emitted a pained, noisy shriek.

The shriek lasted only a split second, because even while the first knife was being thrown by the right hand, the assassin's left hand was moving to the back of his belt, removing another knife, and with an identical throwing motion, winging the knife toward the spot on the tree where the squirrel futilely moved his legs.

That knife too made a lazy half-turn before the spike-sharp point buried itself into the squirrel's small skull, cracking it with an audible split and pinning the animal to the tree. The shriek died in the animal's throat. The assassin smiled and walked toward the tree to retrieve and clean his knives and return them to the belt of six he wore.

But the assassin's smile was not a smile of pleasure. This had been his third squirrel of the day and he felt a lingering tinge of apprehension that his ancestors who had honed this knife-throwing art over the centuries would be disturbed if they could see that he kept his skills sharp by killing squirrels.

But soon, he thought, soon came Wesley Pruiss.

But even that did not give him much satisfaction, for a normal man was not much more to him than a squirrel. No more of a challenge. No more of a threat.

He wished instead for the days he had read about and heard about, in centuries past, when great killers were sent out to track down other great killers.

Today, he thought to his dismay, there were no great killers left to test him and to challenge his genius in a contest in which second-place meant death.

Wesley Pruiss was sleeping when the pickets arrived. Rev. Higbe Muckley wore a long frock coat and a shirt with a frayed collar and a tie whose back strand was longer than the front.

Behind him were forty pickets, most of them carrying signs. One sign read: "Rock of Ages."

"What the hell does that sign mean?" Remo asked Theodosia.

She came to the window and brushed her body against his, but she did not recoil at the touch. Instead, she stayed there and pressed against him harder.

"What sign?" she asked, looking down.

"The one the lunatic is carrying."

"Be more specific."

"'Rock of Ages,'" Remo said. "What does that mean?"

Theodosia shrugged, a rubbing shrug that manipulated her body against Remo's.

Pruiss woke up as the pickets, marching slowly around the building, began to sing.

"What's going on out there?" he snarled from his bed.

"The dancing girls have arrived," Remo said.

"Chase 'em, I'm trying to sleep."

Their voices drifted up from below:

". . . Cleft for me,

83

Let me hide myself in Thee."

"Who brought the pickets?" Pruiss asked sleepily.

"It looks like that Reverend Muckley," Theodosia said. "The bible thumper from California." She pressed closer to Remo.

"Well, at least it ain't none of them lesbian libbers," Pruiss said, before turning his face away on the pillow and closing his eyes. Remo felt Theodosia's body stiffen slightly.

"Why'd this Reverend Muckley come here?" Remo said.

Theodosia said, with sureness. "Those goddam oil companies must have put him up to it. I think they're behind everything that goes on around here."

Pruiss, on the edge of sleep, mumbled something.

"What, Wesley?" Theodosia asked. But Pruiss was asleep.

"The CIA," Remo said.

"What?"

"He said 'the CIA.'"

The dark-haired woman shook her head. Her hair brushed against Remo's cheek.

"Ever since *Gross* did an article on CIA assassins, Wesley's been convinced the CIA is after him. If his car runs out of gas, it's the CIA. If the tailor rips a button off his shirt, it's the CIA. It's like a fixation with him."

"I don't know," Remo said. "They do some strange things."

"If they wanted to harass somebody, they could surely find a better target than Wesley," she said.

"They've got enough people to harass everybody," Remo said.

Downstairs, the hymn-singing had changed to chanting:

ONE, TWO, DOSEY-DO,
PRUISS IS GONE
AND *GROSS* MUST GO.

"That's enough of them," Theodosia said. "I'm calling the police."

"Don't bother," said Remo. "I'll shoo them."

Remo went downstairs and waited on the front steps for Rev. Higbe Muckley to make the circuit of the country club building.

"Nice sign, mama," he said to an old woman who walked by, carrying a placard that read: "We will not be bought off by a mess of tax pottage."

"You think so?" she asked, her bitter lined face lighting up.

"Best one yet," Remo said.

"Think it'll make that Pruiss go home? Back to New York where he belongs?" she asked.

"No," Remo said. "Of course not. Signs never do anything except get you on television."

"Oh my, television." Her hand moved to smooth her hair.

"Absolutely," Remo said. "You're a shoo-in for it."

"You're one of them, aren't you," the woman asked Remo. She nodded toward the house.

"Guess so."

"Well, you probably can't help it, being Italian and all," the woman said.

"Nice talking to you, mother," Remo said as he saw Reverend Muckley come around the far corner of the building, moving his hands as if an orchestra leader, conducting the chants. He was a big man and he ambled along and Remo thought all he needed was a beard and top hat to look like Abraham Lincoln.

Remo fell in alongside him as he passed the steps.

"Good to welcome you here, son," Muckley said. "Where's your sign?"

"I don't have one," Remo said. "Look. There's a man sick upstairs. Whether you like him or not, he's sick. Now why don't you go away and give him a chance to heal up?"

"An angel of the devil," Muckley said. "Sent to visit evil upon us. It is God's will that he be ill and God's will that we be here, the hosts of the Lord, to guard against him." His voice was impassioned but Remo saw there was no fire in Muckley's eyes. He was just reciting from memory, probably something he'd recited hundreds of times before.

"I'm glad we had this little chance to talk," Remo said. He grabbed Muckley's right hand and pinched the flesh between his index and middle fingers. "Sure I can't convince you?"

Muckley winced. "Of course, there is a time and place for Christian charity. Even to those who offend us."

"Right," Remo said. "Sort of turn the other cheek."

"Correct," Muckley said. Remo was leading him away from the house now, back toward the narrow street. As if they were mountain climbers, attached to their leader by lifelines, the forty pickets followed him.

Remo kept pressing the flesh between Muckley's fingers.

"Go away now, Reverend."

"Yes. I understand your point of view."

"I thought you might," Remo said.

"Folks, we've done what we can here," Muckley called out.

There was a groan from the crowd. The old woman shouted, "The television ain't arrived yet."

"Now we should all go back to our homes and pray for this evil man," Muckley said.

"Let's set the house afire," someone else called.

"No, no, no," Muckley yelled. "Christian love will conquer all. Our prayers are the only flames we need. They will light the fire of decency, even in such a cold heart as Westport Prune's."

"Good going." Remo said.

"You going to be here tomorrow?" Muckley asked.

"Every day," Remo said.

"All right," Muckley said. "But no more with the hand, huh?"

"If you behave," Remo said.

He let Muckley's hand go and the tall minister walked off down the road, followed by the straggling line of disappointed picketers.

CHAPTER SIX

The first solar heating equipment arrived early that evening at Furlong County Airport, a paved area that looked like a Grand Union parking lot, three miles from the country club.

Because he had decided to go ahead with the solar program at the urging of Rachmed Baya Bam, Pruiss had insisted the Indian accompany them to the airport to inspect the arrival.

Pruiss rode in the back of an ambulance commandeered from the Furlong County General Hospital for the occasion, and Rachmed Baya Bam helped roll him down the ramps in his wheel chair.

Four ten-foot-high piles of solar panels had arrived aboard a transport plane and now sat on lifts near the far edge of the runway. The hangar floodlights had been turned on to illuminate the black Plexiglass collectors.

"Looks like junk to me," Pruiss said to Theodosia. "How do they work?"

"The sun beats on the black Plexiglass. It absorbs

heat and passes it on to pipes below that hold water. Then the water's circulated through the radiators or whatever and heat the house." She waved at the piles of panels. "And this is just the first, Wesley."

She was walking alongside Pruiss while Baya Bam was wheeling him along. Remo saw her step was light and bouncy. Chiun was next to Remo, his eyes searching the darkness around the hangar.

Baya Bam stopped Pruiss's wheelchair five feet from the piles and stepped to the side to look around.

"Even science pays glorious homage to the sun," he said.

He looked spellbound. All Remo saw was piles of plastic.

Theodosia took the Indian's place behind Pruiss's wheelchair and began to roll it away from the piles.

"Rachmed," she said sharply to the Indian who stood near the piles. "Be careful. They may fall over on you."

He smiled at her, as if inviting her to bask in the salad oil of his warmth. "It is all right, Missss," the said. "I am very agile and will . . ."

"I said stand clear," Theodosia said sharply, "before you get hurt." She kept wheeling Pruiss away. He was twenty feet now from the piles of collectors. Baya Bam shrugged and followed her.

Remo turned to speak to Chiun, but paused for a moment. Something registered on his hearing. There were always sounds in a place but the trained ear could focus on them and out of a hubbub pick the hub and the bub. There was something now fighting for recognition in Remo's ears.

Chiun had heard it too. His head was cocked like that of a deer in the forest, tilted at a slight angle, all

90

the intensity of his tiny body tuning in on his hearing.

Remo began to speak when suddenly Chiun moved forward. To Theodosia, he seemed to drift, but somehow he was moving with an unbelievable speed. At that moment, Remo recognized the sound he had heard too. It was a hissing, sputtering, metallic burning.

He followed after Chiun who tossed himself across Wesley Pruiss's wheelchair and pushed it back toward the hangar farther away from the piles of collector plates. Remo wrapped Theodosia in one arm and scooped up Rachmed in the other and the force of his forward motion carried them back toward the hangar where Chiun was still shielding Pruiss with his body.

There was a split second in time in which the sputtering ended, the hissing stopped, and then there was a roar as an explosion blew away under one of the piles of collectors. There was the cracking sound of plexiglass snapping and behind him as he veered around the corner of the hangar wall, Remo felt heat and pressure, but then they were all behind the wall as all the piles of panels blew up, spraying glass shards and bits of metal into the air. It rocked the corner of the hangar building behind which they stood, Chiun again looking as placid as if he had just returned from meditating in his garden.

Glass and metal pieces dropped, with pinging sounds, on the corrugated metal roof of the building, then slid down and landed about their feet. Theodosia looked stunned; Rachmed Baya Bam cringed in the corner of the building behind her.

Pruiss had his usual angry look on his face.

"What the Christ is? . . ."

"A boom," said Chiun.

91

"Bomb," said Remo.

"Those fucking oil companies," spat Theodosia.

She stepped out now from behind the hangar and looked at the runway, covered with fragments of plexiglass, glinting sharply black in the reflection of the runway lights.

Airport workers were running from the hangar and Pruiss said, "Let's get out of here."

"Is it safe yet?" asked Baya Bam, still cowering in the corner.

"Yes, it's safe," Theodosia said. She grabbed Pruiss's wheelchair and began pushing it rapidly back toward the ambulance. Rachmed raced ahead and ran into the ambulance, hiding in a far corner.

Remo and Chiun looked at the wreckage.

"Close call," Remo said.

Chiun nodded.

"So much for knives with horses on them," Remo said. "No assassin works with a knife, then with a bomb."

Chiun continued to look at the pile of rubble.

"Perhaps," he said. "Perhaps."

CHAPTER SEVEN

By the time their ambulance had reached the Pruiss residence, Theodosia had decided. She was keeping the other three bodyguards on the payroll. She twisted her hands together nervously as she told Remo.

"That's not necessary," Remo said.

"No," said Chiun. "Not necessary. If you have money to throw away, I know this nice little village where the people . . ."

"Chiun," said Remo.

Theodosia shook her head. Dark curls splashed around her shoulders.

"No. This is the way I want it. I'll just sleep better."

"Suit yourself," Remo said. "Just keep them out of our way."

"You do it," she said. "I don't want to deal with anybody tonight."

Remo had the three bodyguards meet him in the old ground floor golf pro shop of the former country club.

They came in as if expecting an ambush, scanning

the room cautiously with their eyes, glancing behind the glass counter and the doors.

Remo was practice putting with a putter he had pulled from a sample bag of clubs.

"Nobody hiding in the golf bags either," he said, looking up.

"Now listen, Yank, what's this all about?" the mercenary colonel said. "We're supposed to be on duty." He was a husky man with a mustache twirled into points so precise that only a sadist would have inflicted that kind of discipline on his facial hair.

The small arms expert and the karate man nodded.

"Theodosia's decided to keep you on," Remo said. "Don't ask me why."

"The 'why' is because we're the best there is," the colonel said.

"Sure," Remo said. "Right." He putted a ball across the room and stopped it twelve feet away on a little dark spot in the green rug. Pro shops always had green rugs, he realized. "Anyway, I just wanted to tell you to stay out of our way. Work outside or something." He inspected the soft rubber grip of the putter.

"Do you know what a drag it is being able to one-putt every green?" he said. "I liked golf better when I used to miss a shot once in a while."

"You know, Yank," the colonel said with a faint sneer. "When this is all over . . ."

"If you guard yourselves the way you guarded Pruiss in that hospital," Remo said, "when this is all over, you'll be lucky to be alive."

"You Americans are always pushy," the colonel said. He fingered the stock of his submachine gun. "When this is over, just you and me."

Remo smiled at him, then putted another ball

across the floor. It stopped, touching the first practice putt.

"You don't seem worried, Yank," the colonel said.

"I told you," Remo said. "I never miss. One putt all the time."

"I'm not talking about your bleeding golf game," the colonel said. "I'm talking about big things. Life and death."

"If you want something big, you ought to try a twenty-dollar Nassau with presses on the back nine," Remo said.

"Life and death," the colonel insisted. "You know how many men I've killed?"

Remo putted another ball. It stopped touching the first two.

"I've seen what you killed," Remo said. "Untrained ninnies who couldn't tie their own shoes. People who signed up to be soldiers so they could eat anybody they captured. The Cubans are probably the worst fighters in the world, except for the French, and when they got to Africa, they kicked your ass and sent all you make-believe field marshals home."

The colonel took a step forward and put his foot in the line of Remo's putt.

Remo dropped another ball on the floor and putted it across the carpet, with a chopping up and down stroke. The ball squirted off the putter head and skidded across the floor. When it reached the colonel's shoe, the back english took effect and the ball hopped into the air, over the shoe, and stopped dead still on the far side, next to the three other balls.

"Will you put that bloody putter down?" the colonel snarled.

"Don't have to," Remo said.

The colonel growled in anger, reached down and

95

snatched one of the golf balls from the carpet. He flung it across the ten feet of space separating himself and Remo. The white, rock-hard ball sped in on Remo's face. He turned his body slightly toward the left and raised his left hand in a buzz-saw motion. The ball was intercepted by Remo's hand. It hit the hand without a sound and seemed to hang on the side of Remo's open palm for a moment. Then he dropped his hand and two halves of the golf ball fell to the floor, sliced neatly in two as if by a surgical laser beam.

The three men looked at the golf ball in shock.

"Guard outside," Remo said again softly.

They turned toward the door.

"Colonel," Remo said. The mercenary officer, his face drained of color, turned to meet Remo's eyes.

"That was a good ball," Remo said. "A Titleist DT. I'm docking your account a dollar thirty-five."

Theodosia had put Remo in a bedroom on one side of Wesley Pruiss and Chiun in a room on the other. Her room was down past Remo's and Rachmed Baya Bam's was the farthest down the corridor.

When Remo got upstairs, the Indian had already gone to bed because he said his nerves had been shattered by the American propensity for violence. He could easily, sirrr, have been killed before his mission in life had been accomplished.

Chiun hissed to Remo, "That means as long as there is still a dollar loose in this country."

Theodosia had put Pruiss to sleep and Remo and Chiun headed for their separate rooms.

"Which one of you is staying with Wesley?" she asked.

"I don't like sharing a bed," Chiun said. "I sleep on my mat."

"But somebody's got to stay in his room," she said. She looked at Remo helplessly.

"No, we don't," Remo said. "Nobody can get within a hundred feet of this room without us knowing it. Don't worry about it." She did not look convinced.

"Look, if you want to do something," Remo said, "pull down the shades in his bedroom. If that makes you feel better."

When she came back out of Pruiss's room, she told Remo: "You forgot your weapons."

"No, we didn't."

"Where are they?"

"They're always with us," Remo said.

"Show me," Theodosia said.

"They're secret," Remo said. He stuffed his hands into the pockets of his black chinos.

"Let me have a good night's sleep," she said. "What kind of weapons do you use?"

Chiun paused at his bedroom door.

"The most deadly weapons known to mankind," he said. He went inside. Theodosia looked at Remo.

"The same weapons we used to get through those steel windows at the hospital," Remo said.

"You've brought them?"

"Yes. Never travel without them," Remo said.

Theodosia looked at him suspiciously. "You're sure you can tell if Wesley's in any danger?"

"Sure I'm sure. If it makes you feel any better, I'll sleep with my door open tonight."

He smiled and she shrugged.

"I hope you're worth what I'm paying you," she said. She sounded sure he wasn't.

He took his hands from his pockets and held her

soft hands in his, stroking the knuckles with his thumbs.

"More," he said. "Go to sleep. It's been a long day."

Almost reluctantly, she started down the hall, then stopped and went back to Pruiss's room and peeked inside.

"He's sleeping," she told Remo.

"Good," said Remo.

"I want you to kill anybody who tries to go into that room tonight," she said sternly.

"You got it," Remo said. "Go to sleep."

He entered his own room, undressed and lay on the bed. There had been a time, years before, when he had had trouble sleeping. Going to bed was just another struggle in a day filled with struggles and he would turn and toss on his bed until his drained and exhausted body reluctantly accepted sleep.

But that had been years ago, back before CURE, back before Chiun had transformed him into something different by giving him control of his own body, able to make it do what he wanted it to do.

He had once mentioned the change in his sleeping habits to Chiun, who laughed one of his infrequent laughs.

"You have always been asleep," Chiun had said.

When Remo finally came to understand the gifts Chiun had given him, he reflected that the ancient Korean was correct. He had been asleep, never in touch with his body. Most men used only a small fraction of their bodies and an even smaller fraction of their senses. Remo was man pushed toward the ultimate, using almost all his body, almost all his senses. And Chiun? Chiun *was* the ultimate. The secrets of centuries of Sinanju were stored in his mind and body and it explained why that frail old man, less than five feet tall, weighing under a hundred pounds, could bring physical forces to bear that had to be seen, and still were disbelieved.

Now, for Remo, sleeping was just another function of living and Remo was in control of those functions. He slept when he wanted to and for as long as he wanted to and the totality of rest he twisted from sleep was so great that a few minutes rest to him was the same as hours of sleep to a normal man.

And to go to sleep was the simplest thing of all. It did not require consciously willing the body to sleep. It simply meant letting the body do the natural thing, which was to sleep. "A lion never has insomnia," Chiun had once said. Sleeping became a thing done more by instinct than by conscious desire. But Remo controlled the instinct.

He thought of none of these things as he lay on the bed, because one moment he was awake, and the next moment he was asleep. Not the "little death" of sleep that most men suffered through. Because Remo lived a life without tensions racking his mind and body, because he was not in conflict with himself during the day, he did not have to escape that conflict at night in the deep coma that most people called rest.

Thirty minutes later he heard it and was fully awake. There was a sound in the hall. Chiun too would have heard it, he knew.

Remo moved quietly from the bed toward the open door of his room. The sound was footsteps, soft footsteps. It was someone barefooted moving down the thick carpeting of the hallway, and while to most people the movement would have been soundless, that was only because they were used to listening to the hard clicks of hard shoes on hard floors. Anything less than that was silent. But Remo could hear the soft crinkle of the wool carpet as it was pressed down by the bare feet stepping along it, and then the slight release as the foot lifted and took the next step. It was a hissing sound. The footsteps were coming closer to him. He heard no sound of clothing rustling.

A small person. Perhaps five-foot-six or seven. One hundred and seventeen pounds. Long legged. Chiun seemed to know something about the person who had thrown a knife into Wesley Pruiss's back. Did that make the assassin an Oriental? Remo wondered. An Oriental might fit the physical description of the person coming slowly and softly down the hallway toward Remo's room. Toward Pruiss's room.

Remo waited until the steps were only three feet from his open door and then walked out into the hallway.

Staring up at him was Theodosia. She was dressed only in white panties and bra. She looked up at Remo in surprise.

"What are you doing?" he asked.

"I was testing you," she said. "Just to see if you were on the job."

Remo shook his head. "You'll never know how lucky you are."

"Why?"

"Because you gave instructions to kill anybody trying to enter Pruiss's room. If you had touched the knob on that door, Chiun would have put you away before you could blink." Without raising his voice, Remo said, "It's all right, Chiun. It's Theodosia. Go back to sleep."

The faint Oriental voice squeaked back from inside Chiun's room. "Sleep? How can I sleep with herds of elephants thundering down the hall at all hours of the

100

night? I will never get any rest on this job. Woe is me."

"Come on in here," Remo said. "Unless you want to hear him kvetch all night." He led Theodosia into his room and closed the door behind them.

"I thought I was being very quiet," she said. She seemed not at all self-conscious about wearing nothing but her lingerie.

"You were," he said. "Most people wouldn't have heard you."

"You did."

"We're not most people," Remo said. He realized Theodosia was standing close to him, her body pressed against his. She seemed so small, so vulnerable that he lifted up her chin with his hand and leaned over to kiss her on the mouth.

Her lips stiffened momentarily, then relaxed and were rich and pulpy as they slid against Remo's. He moved his hands down her bare back, which felt smooth and oiled, and toyed with the elastic waistband of her nylon panties. Theodosia pressed against him with the middle of her body and clapped her arms about his neck.

She released her lips, leaned her head back and smiled at him.

"What's a nice guy like you doing in a place like this?" she asked.

"Just lucky, I guess," said Remo, drawing her close to his body again by wrapping his arms around her bare back.

He allowed his body to stir and when it did, he remembered how pleasant it had once been. It was all too easy for him now and he would never recapture the lustful joys of scoring when scoring was hard to do. Still the woman in his arms pleasured him. He fiddled with the little metallic clip on the back of Theodosia's bra but couldn't open it, just as he had never been able to open them, so he nipped the elastic strap between his right thumb and index finger and with a small twist of his hand, broke the elastic in two. The bra slid down the front of Theodosia's chest as she shrugged her shoulders and Remo felt her hard-pointed breasts touch his chest.

He raised a hand to her breast and she pressed her lips against him again, hard, demanding, insistent, and pushed him backwards toward the bed. He felt her fingers slide against the muscled flesh of his hard stomach and her long fingernails traced lazy circles about his navel.

She wore a sweet perfume but it was sweet with the smell of the outdoors and not with the sweet of sugar and chemicals. It wafted into Remo's nostrils and he savored the aroma as he let her body carry him down onto the bed. She was feverishly clawing at the waistband of his undershorts and Remo said,

"Easy, easy. What's the hurry?"

"Easy, my ass," Theodosia said and somehow twirling around on the bed, she had both their undergarments off and she was climbing over him.

Even though he did not want it to happen, it had become too much a part of him to ignore and Remo remembered all the steps ingrained in him by Chiun's training, and without thinking of them, he went from step one to step two to step three.

Chiun had taught him twenty-seven progressive steps for sex. Chiun had called it a beginner's course "but adequate for most of your needs, especially since you whites rut like cows in a field." Twenty-seven steps and Remo had never found a woman with

102

whom he could get past Step 13 before she was turned into a flesh-covered mass of quivering jelly.

Theodosia moved around Remo as he went through the steps, the pressure touch on the small of the back, the fingernail scrape three inches from the center of an armpit, the tug and release of the small hairs at the back of her neck. He felt guilty about getting ready to turn the woman into jelly, but he knew nothing else to do in sex now except the things he had been taught. He wondered for a moment if Theodosia's continuous exposure to rampant, kinky sex at *Gross* magazine and as Pruiss's mistress might somehow render her immune to his processes.

He performed Step 13, deciding to use the left elbow instead of the right, but there was no visible response from the woman and for the first time, he moved to Step 14, involving both his hands and the inside of his right ankle and the back of Theodosia's left knee.

He paused, waiting for her to scream in a paroxysm of ecstasy.

She smiled down at him and said, "You're tickling me."

Remo lay back on the bed, for a moment totally relaxed, and then went on to Steps 15 and 16 and 17. At 18, Theodosia began to purr and he got all the way to step 22 before they joined together in a mingling outpouring of warm wet bliss that left Theodosia apparently dazed and Remo relaxed and calm, lying naked on his back on the bed.

Gallantly, he said "Congratulations."

"For what? You're not going to tell me I rescued you from homosexuality are you?"

She was already sitting up in bed, almost businesslike, as if the passion of the last few minutes had had nothing to do with her. He wondered at her resiliency.

"You're kind of remarkable," he said.

"Aren't you nice to say that?" she said. "Ah owes it all to living clean, eating right and going to bed early."

"And often," Remo said.

Theodosia laughed. "All right. Going to bed early and often. You're not exactly untrained yourself, Where'd you learn all those things you were doing?"

"It's a long story," Remo said.

"I've got time, now that I know Wesley's in good hands," Theodosia said.

Remo changed the subject. "What about Wesley? I guess we keep this our little secret. I can't stand jealous lovers."

"Lovers? Jealous? Wesley?" Theodosia broke into a long full-throated laugh.

"What's so funny? You are Wesley's woman, aren't you?"

"Sure I'm Wesley's woman. I handle the books. I handle the business. I advise him on business and investments. I do the labor negotiations for *Gross.* That's it."

"That's it? You mean that Wesley would let a natural resource like you go to waste?"

"Dear one," she said. "Wesley's impotent. He can't make it. That's why he keeps me around all the time. I'm his excuse for not performing with somebody else."

"What a shame," Remo said.

"It is. More than you know. He was like anybody else when he was driving up. But when he got to the top with money and power and women climbing all over him, his sex drive vanished. To tell you the

104

truth, I think sometimes he's a little bit happy about that assassin's knife 'cause it gives him an excuse not to have to perform."

"And you know how many men in America dream of being in his shoes?" Remo said.

"And do you know how many times he wishes he were in the shoes of some drunken truckdriver who swills beer all night and then comes home and cops the wife's nookie?" Theodosia said. She fumbled in the drawer of the end table next to the bed and found a pack of cigarettes. She lit one and lay back next to Remo, inhaling deeply.

"You know, I saw the first issue of *Gross*," Remo said. "You and the bull?"

"Funny. I wouldn't have picked you to be a Gro-Gru," she said.

"'Gro-Gru'?" Remo asked.

"Grossie-Groupie. A reader."

"No," Remo said. "I was waiting for a man. He wasn't home yet. He had a copy of the magazine on his desk. I read it until he came."

"If he had a desk, he doesn't sound like one of our readers either."

"Yeah," Remo said, remembering. "He had a desk. I left him in one of the drawers. Anyway, I remembered you. But with a bull?"

"It gave me good training for you," Theodosia said. She dragged again on the cigarette and put her hand on Remo's thigh. "Only fooling. It's all posed."

"Even posed," Remo said. "How the hell'd you get involved in that? What goes through your mind when you know you're going to have the picture published and your family and all's going to see it?"

"Half the models are hookers who aren't junked up yet." Theodosia said. "The others who do the freaky

105

stuff *want* everybody to see it. It's a way of getting even. Most of them were rejected kids and now they just want to show everybody what they were missing when they rejected them. They're just working out their problems. If you're Jewish and rich, you go to a shrink. If you can't handle that, but you're good-looking enough, you can pose naked with a bull."

"So you did that and then what?"

"I was Wesley's first girl. He had a little three-man operation then. So I asked for a job and he found out I could do more than just flash at a camera. And then a little later, he started to have his problems so I was good camouflage for him too. So I hung on and survived and now I run everything for him."

"So who's trying to kill him?" Remo said.

Theodosia let out a long puff of smoke. It battled, futilely, in Remo's senses with her perfume, then lost. She still smelled sweet.

"Those goddamn oil companies," she said. "We started hearing a lot of crap right after Wesley said he was going to do that solar energy thing out here. I wouldn't put it past them. That's why I hired all you people."

She stubbed out her cigarette in an ashtray and rolled over onto her side, toward Remo. Her right breast rested on his left bicep.

"Enough talk," she said. "Get busy. What do you think I pay you for?"

The assassin stood in the shadow of the trees behind the practice putting green of the country club.

It would be easy, he thought, as he watched the mercenary colonel march up and down in front of the entrance to the building, carrying his submachine gun, carefully checking to his left, to his right, behind him, over and over again, a narrow military man carrying out a narrow military operation.

There was this one here. The karate expert had the left side of the house and half of the back. The right side and the other half of the back of the building was being patrolled by the small arms expert.

The assassin had been told there were two new bodyguards, an old Oriental and a young American. They were probably inside the house. Just as well; he would deal with them later. First things first.

The assassin moved out of the shadows, cleared his throat, then slowly slipped behind a tree.

The colonel looked up at the noise and saw a figure moving behind a tree.

He went into a combat crouch and began moving across the putting green toward the spot he had seen the movement. But the assassin was already moving away from there, circling around to his left, and when the colonel approached the tree and extended his weapon toward it, the assassin was behind him.

He looked across the twelve feet separating them. He pulled a silver-bladed knife from the back of his belt and raised it over his head. His hand flashed down. This time, there was no calculated near miss. The knife burrowed into the back of the soldier, cutting through his clothes, flesh, muscles and severing his spinal cord. The colonel dropped without uttering a sound. His machine gun made a faint little *thwop* when it hit the night-dampened grass of the forest floor.

The assassin paused only long enough to retrieve his knife. He wiped it clean on fallen leaves, returned it to his belt, and moved across the putting green to the front door of the country club. There he waited in the shadows of the two large columns flanking the front door.

The guards were in a rhythm and the karate expert would be first. He had watched them. Every sixth time they prowled their section of the perimeter of the grounds, they came to the front porch to check. And they staggered the count so that the karate expert came first, then three rounds later, the small arms master, and three rounds later, the karate expert. Over and over.

The assassin had watched them for hours. His tradition was to know his enemy, because knowledge was not only power, knowledge was death. The assassin had also watched the shades pulled over the windows in Wesley Pruiss's room and he had caught through one of the uncovered hall windows a flash of movement in the hallway which seemed to be a woman walking, presumably Pruiss's assistant, since he knew of no other women in the house.

The assassin wore no wristwatch; he had no need of one. Time was a fact of his life and his internal clock never missed a stroke. He could count seconds without a miss up to ten minutes. He could sense the passage of minutes and not be wrong by so much as the tick of a clock at the end of the day.

He did not have to count here, however, to know when the karate expert would appear. The end of the house he patrolled was bordered by a heavier kind of grass, and to the assassin's keen senses, heightened by the fact that he was practicing his deadly art, the sound of the martial arts expert's unclad feet moving through that high grass would mean he was ready to turn the corner and check in with the colonel at the front of the building.

He waited in the shadows and listened. The quiet

night roared with sounds. The beasts in the woods near the house chattered ceaselessly to each other. The wind had its own sound and some kinds of birds that flew at night made a different kind of sound as they soared through the air. The house, even though all were abed, was as noisy as if it lived. Water pipes continuously contracted and expanded and creaked gently in the U-brackets that held them to ceiling beams in the cellar. Electric clocks whirred. Radios hummed quietly. Refrigerators kicked on and off automatically. There were few places in the world that were really silent to one who but listened.

The breeze blowing toward the house was cool and had the taste of tree green on it as it reached the assassin. He tasted it on his lips and waited.

Ninety seconds later, he heard the bare footfall touch the high grass, and a moment later, the karate expert turned the corner of the building and looked toward the porch. At that moment, the assassin stepped out from behind the column. Even as he moved, his hands were reaching behind him to his belt. The martial arts expert saw the unfamiliar man and, courageous and foolish, ran across the ground toward him. At ten-feet distance, the assassin threw the knives with both hands simultaneously. At nine feet they struck, one in the throat severing the windpipe, the other slanting between two ribs to pierce the heart muscle. The man dropped with no sound other than that of his body hitting the heavily-matted short grass of the practice green.

Quickly the assassin moved from the porch and removed the knives from the dead body. The man stared at him blankly, his eyes rolling up into his head like a fish dying on a gaffing hook. He recovered his knives, wiped them clean on the white gi of the dead man, then dragged the body across the practice green and into the small stand of trees where he dumped it next to that of the mercenary colonel.

He went back to the porch. The whole killing operation had taken less than two minutes. He no longer tasted the green of the trees on his lips; instead his mind dwelt only on the satisfying thwack of knives hitting target. He saw in his memory the two bodies lying, bloodied, on the ground and for the first time that night, he smiled.

He wanted to do it again. It would be only seconds before the small arms man came around the corner of the building but those seconds ticked in his mind like a clock heading for eternity. He could not wait.

He walked off the porch to the corner of the building. He squatted low as he peered around the corner. The firearms expert was only five feet away, just walking again toward the back of the building. The assassin withdrew another clean, unused knife from his belt. He never liked to use the same knife twice, before using the others. He felt it was wrong not to spread the work equally over all the machinery. Hefting it in his right hand, he stepped out into the short cut grass next to the flower bed.

The firearms expert carried a pistol in his hand so the assassin was silent. He did not want him to get off a shot to alert anyone else. He raised the knife next to his right ear and let fly. The blade bit flesh and the firearms expert dropped. His gun fell uselessly onto the grass. Again the knife was cleaned and the body dragged across the putting green to be deposited with the others.

The assassin walked back across the green. It would be easy to go on, he thought. A houseful of sleeping people. Pruiss. Theodosia. The Indian. The two bodyguards. More blood for his knives.

His hand touched the front doorknob, then released it. It would be nice but it would be unprofessional. He would do what he was paid to do. He walked off back to the woods.

Theodosia slept. Remo had again gone to Step 22 of his 27 but she seemed to climax only when she wanted to climax and it jarred Remo that she had been invulnerable to him.

She slept now on his arm, knowing that Pruiss would not be out of his bed to surprise them together. Remo had reopened the hall door. He was lying in bed, thinking, when he heard a hissing sound.

"Sooooo," came the voice from the door, in a high pitch of indignation.

"Yes, Chiun," Remo said with a sigh.

"Here you lie rutting, as all you people do so well . . ."

"Don't knock it," Remo interrupted. "Step 22 tonight. First time ever."

"I am not interested in the vulgar details of your vulgar activities. Your life is a vulgarity and nothing in it would surprise me," Chiun said. "But perhaps you can spare me a moment so I can tell you something concerning why you are here."

Remo dropped Theodosia from his arm and sat up in bed. Her head hit the pillow with a thud and she woke up also. She looked at Remo, then at Chiun standing in the doorway, wearing his brown sleeping kimono.

"What?" she began to say.

Chiun ignored her. He looked at Remo. "The assassin has been here," he said.

111

Remo looked at him in something close to disbelief.

"Yes, that is right, white thing," Chiun said. "Look at me with your mouth hanging open. While you two were behaving like rabbits in a box, he was here."

"What happened?" Remo asked.

"He did not enter the building. He moved outside. He moved many times in many different directions. He practiced his art. He is gone now."

"Is Wesley all right?" Theodosia asked. She started to get out of bed.

"He is as all right as one can be who has a faithless woman," Chiun said.

"The bodyguards," Remo said.

Chiun raised his hand. "There is nothing to be done tonight," he said. "What has occurred has occurred. We will deal with it tomorrow."

Remo slumped back onto the pillow.

"Now, if you two can find it in yourselves, I would suggest some sleep," said Chiun.

Without even a whisper of sound, he left the room. Theodosia stared at the open door.

"How does he know what happened outside?" she asked.

"Because he is the Master of Sinanju," Remo said. "Go to sleep."

But he did not take his own advice.

CHAPTER EIGHT

When he arrived at the small suite of offices that housed Rev. Higbe Muckley's operation, there was a sign on the inside door.

It read: PLEASE WAIT. COMMUNING WITH GOD.

Inside the inner office, Muckley knelt alongside his secretary. They looked at a cross on the wall.

"Oh, God, their hearts were hardened and they do not hear our message," Muckley said.

"Amen," said his secretary, who kept her back very straight because she had a tendency to fall over when she leaned too far forward.

"Open their hearts to Your goodness, so they will receive our message of the glories of faith," Muckley said. He reached his right hand around the back of his secretary and touched the side of her right breast, through the thin jersey material of her top.

"Amen," she said.

"Why do evildoers persist in the land?" the Reverend Muckley asked the piece of plaster on the wall. He cupped her breast in his right hand and felt its soft weight. It sent a tingle up his right arm as it always did.

"Amen," his secretary said. She leaned fractionally toward the right so all her breast could lay against Muckley's palm. He kneaded the flesh.

"Help us get rid of Pruiss and evil, etcetera etcetera, etcetera and I'll think of more later," Muckley said.

"Amen," the secretary said, as Muckley climbed on her.

"Don't forget 'Hallelujah,' Sister Corinne," Muckley said.

"First you got to give me a hallelujah, Reverend," said his secretary.

"Ask and you shall receive," said Muckley.

"Oh, hallelujah, hallelujah, hallelujah," she said a few moments later.

The Reverend Higbe Muckley, A.B.D., A.C.D., B.C.D., and B.E.D., was sitting behind his desk when his secretary ushered Will Bobbin into the inner office. The letters in his name meant nothing, except trifecta bets he had made and won at the race track in the last several years. His secretary paused in the doorway.

"Type those letters right up, Sister," he said.

"Yes, Doctor," she said. She winked at him, which Bobbin saw in the polished glass door of a wall-mounted bookcase.

He grinned at Muckley who cleared his throat and asked officiously, "Now what can I do for you, Brother Bobbin?"

Bobbin closed the office door.

"It's what I can do for you, Reverend," he said. He twisted the curl of hair over his right temple.

"What did you have in mind?"

114

"You've been bombing out," Bobbin said. "You've been here a couple of days already and nothing but yawns."

"It takes time to bring people to act against evil," Muckley said.

"Hogwash," Bobbin said. "You can't get these people riled up against Pruiss because he's cutting their taxes. That's the truth and you know it and I know it so let's not dawdle over that."

Muckley shrugged. "What do you have in mind, Brother?"

"I've got something that'll wake them up. Something more powerful than taxes. Something that'll get these people steamed and marching, just to make sure Pruiss gets his butt out of town."

"What would that be?" Muckley asked.

"More powerful than money," Bobbin said. "Sex."

Muckley looked up at him sharply.

"Picture this," said Bobbin. "Proof that Pruiss isn't out here for solar energy. He's out here to turn this nice middle-America, hogbelly and pancakes-for-breakfast county into the pornography capital of the United States? How about that?"

"You got proof?" Muckley asked.

"Yes."

"Then we'll get that sucker," Muckley said. "That'll get them marching."

"My idea exactly," Bobbin said.

Muckley searched Bobbin's face and said, after a pause, "I don't know anything about you, Mr. Bobbin."

"That's the way I want it."

"What do you get out of this?"

"Does it really matter?" Bobbin asked. "Can't you believe I'm doing it just to stamp out evil."

"That's fine in fund-raising letters," Muckley said. "But what are you really doing it for?"

"Let's just say I'm going to get out of it everything I want."

Muckley shrugged. "Whatever," he said. "You said something about proof that Pruiss is here to do pornography. You got that proof?"

"It'll be here in the morning plane from New York."

"Bring it in, brother, and let's see what we can do."

As he left the building, Will Bobbin thought that it was incredible that such fools could rise to positions of prominence. Muckley's idea of selling the ministry to allow people to buy at discount was a good idea, and probably the only idea the man had ever had or would ever have. And yet it had been enough to make him a national figure. Will Bobbin would play him like an accordion, to keep the wheels rolling until they rolled right over Wesley Pruiss and his solar energy scheme.

In his office, the Reverend Dr. Higbe Muckley looked at the door that swung closed behind Will Bobbin. It was the oil industry. He was sure of it. Who else had a vested interest in driving Wesley Pruiss out of Furlong County? Well, there was no law that prevented the oil industry from doing God's work. Or Higbe Muckley's.

He would wait to see what kind of proof arrived on the morning plane.

Chiun walked across the neat grass of the practice green toward the small stand of trees, beyond which the land sloped down a deep hill, across the eighteenth fairway, and to a forest beyond.

Remo followed him. "You know where they are?" he asked.

116

Chiun, wordlessly, pointed to two faint sets of parallel lines trailing across the green. Remo recognized them as probably heel marks from two bodies dragged over the grass.

Chiun stopped and looked behind a large tree. Remo saw the bodies of the three bodyguards, neatly piled up.

"Beautiful work," Chiun said.

"I don't know," Remo said stubbornly. "I think weapons take the fun out of it."

"Fun?" said Chiun. "What is this? What I teach you now is fun?"

"You know what I mean," Remo said.

"Yes, I do," Chiun said. "You are right. Weapons weaken the art. But at least if one is to use them, he should use them well. Our assassin uses his knives well. See. Here. Two men, dispatched perfectly with one thrust each. And here . . . ," He pointed to the body of the martial arts expert, ". . . here two knives were used. One to kill and one to prevent an outcry."

Chiun touched the body with his toe.

"You still think they're red handled knives with horses engraved on the blades?" Remo asked.

Chiun shook his head. "That is not a think. That is a know. And that is what makes this dangerous."

"Well, Pruiss is lucky. He's got us."

"I am not talking about this Pruiss. It is dangerous for you," Chiun said.

"Why me?" asked Remo, but Chiun had already started to walk away.

They went back to the practice green where Pruiss lay in the portable bed, spun around so that the sun shone in his eyes. Rachmed Baya Bam had lifted the covers over Pruiss's legs again and was intoning words to the sun, in a language Remo did not understand. Theodosia looked at him approvingly. She glanced at Remo as he and Chiun returned and she smiled. Remo smiled back. Chiun sniffed.

The thin hissing voice of Rachmed Baya Bam insinuated itself over the clearing as he kneaded the useless legs of Wesley Pruiss.

"What language is that, Chiun?" Remo asked.

"Hindi," Chiun said.

"You understand it?"

"Yes. Even though he speaks it badly."

"What's he saying?" Remo asked.

"He is saying 'Oh, sun. Oh, yes, sun. This is Rachmed, sun. You hear me, sun? I'm talking to you, sun. Where are you, sun? Shine on me, sun. I don't want to sunburn though, sun, so don't shine too hard. How you like it up there, sun? Do you ever get bored, going around in circles, sun?' "

"C'mon, Chiun."

"You asked, I answered. What you do with truth is no concern of mine," Chiun said.

Pruiss cried out and Remo glanced over. Rachmed seemed to be wrestling with the muscles of Pruiss's right thigh.

"I felt it, I felt it," Pruiss said.

Theodosia squealed. "Wesley, I knew it. I knew it."

Baya Bam said in English, "Thank you, sun, oh gracious orb, whose gift is love and whose wisdom is in understanding."

"I think I can move it," Pruiss said. "My right leg. I think I can move it. Look. See if I can move it, Theo. Look."

The woman leanded over. "A little," she said, but her voice was doubting. "Maybe I saw it move a little."

"I know it moved," Pruiss said. "I know it did."

"Thank you, gracious sun," said Baya Bam.

"I think that's enough, Rachmed," said Theodosia. "Wesley needs his pain medicine. Let's get him inside."

Baya Bam nodded. Theodosia came to Remo.

"What did you find?" she asked.

"Bodyguards all dead. Knives," Remo said.

"That man is a fraud," Chiun told Theodosia.

"Thank you," she said coldly. "But he seems to be helping, doesn't he? All dead?"

"Yes," Remo said.

"Do you think we need more help?" she asked.

Remo shook his head. "We'll just wait for the twerp with the knives to surface. He will eventually."

Theodosia saw Rachmed wheeling the bed away.

"I've got to give Wesley his medicine right away," she said.

Remo watched her walk away.

"Frigid, I guess," he said. "But she's really dedicated to that Pruiss."

"She makes sure that she gives him his medicine on time," Chiun said.

"That's what I said," Remo said.

"No, it's not," said Chiun.

Before Flamma had been Flamma, she had been Blow-Blow La Flume She had been the "special projects editor" for a New York publishing house. Her most special project had been the publisher who hired her and their in-office couplings had been long, complicated, frequent and so messy that when the publisher finally went to jail for child molestation, the couch in his office had been neither kept nor sold. The new publishers had taken it downstairs and burned it at curbside. The smell lingered on the New York street for days afterward. Blow-Blow La Flume was fired with the couch.

Still the whole experience had been a step up from the massage parlor for Blow-Blow, who, after his passing, had invested the publisher with all the virtues imagination could create, even though people who dealt with him on a less personal level had tended to regard him as a particularly virulent form of saprophytic fungus.

It was an easy step from the publisher's office to *Gross Magazine*, which was just getting off the ground. Blow-Blow's greatest virtue was that she had none—she would do anything. Theodosia had done the first centerfold for Wesley Pruiss, but Flamma did the next three, wearing disguises. so she couldn't be recognized as the same model. It was Pruiss who changed her name to Flamma, which, he said, had a classy ring. He also had her work out the techniques for belly-dancing with sterno burning in her navel. This was not as hard as it seemed, because the problem wasn't heat, it was cold. Sterno burned almost like an evaporation-with-flame, and an evaporating substance chills the surface beneath it. Flamma's navel was so cold at times that she was afraid to go to her belly-dancing lessons for fear that she would crack wide open in a sudden lunge of activity.

Wesley Pruiss was impressed by her experience in publishing and assigned her the task of entertaining distributors, printers and buyers to whom he owed money. She did this generally by letting them buy her a drink and then insisting they go to bed with her right away, because she couldn't live another moment without their bodies.

At first she had tried to talk to several of them but

they wanted to talk about things like gross revenues and print orders and return percentages and profit and loss statements and all she ever remembered from her first job was seeing the publisher write things on the inside of a match book. He told her they were profit and loss statements. He would spend an entire dinner in a restaurant, rubbing her legs under the table with his, while putting numbers inside a match-book, and when they left the restaurant, he would leave the matchbook on the table.

Flamma had a dream. Even before she had been Blow-Blow La Flume she had been movie-struck, and she badgered Pruiss to start a film division and make movies, and if he had been seduceable, she would have tried that too. But Wesley had never shown any real interest in her and besides Theodosia seemed to have her hooks in him and never let the two of them spend any real time alone. Finally, Pruiss had said he would make a film and Flamma had thought of a re-make of the life of Mata Hari or something like that. She saw herself as Greta Garbo. She saw the interviews in which she explained she was born in Ankara, Turkey, of a family of great wealth and stature. She saw herself winning awards at Cannes. She saw herself crowding Candice Bergen and Rex Reed out of the headlines.

When Pruiss told her that the movie was going to be called *Animal Instincts* and was would involve a *ménage à ménagerie*, she was only slightly crushed. After all, even Greta Garbo had to start somewhere. From there, it would be onward and upward.

And then, just like that, the movie plans had been dropped. Theodosia explained to her on the telephone that it was because Wesley had been crippled and couldn't think of movies now, but Flamma knew better. She knew the bitch had deep-sixed Flamma's future because of jealousy, trying to keep her from the stardom that should be hers, and when Will Bobbin approached her, she hadn't even cared about the money. But when he promised her a film test at a Hollywood studio owned mostly by oil money, she quickly agreed to blow the whistle on Wesley Pruiss and his plans to create a dirty film center in Furlong County. She felt no remorse. A girl had to start looking out for herself sometime.

Bobbin met her plane when it landed at the Furlong County Airport. Flamma looked around through enormous circular sunglasses and was a little disappointed when she saw no one resembling a newsman or press agent. She had prepared for the occasion by figuring out a costume that was both mysterious and provocative. She wore a trench coat (mysterious) and under it, she was naked (provocative). She could go either way as the occasion demanded.

"Now, listen," Bobbin said as they drove toward town in his rented car.

"That's what I hate about not being a star yet," Flamma said.

"What's that?"

"People are always saying 'now, listen' to me. Do you think they said that to Marilyn Monroe?"

"Not if she listened. Anyway, sorry. I want you to meet this Reverend Muckley. He's the one who's going to blow the whistle on Pruiss for us."

"Who is he?"

"He's a mail order fraud of a minister from California. But he's got a lot of money, he's always on the television and he'll get you and your story in every paper and on every television broadcast from coast to coast. Instant stardom. And then the silver screen."

Flamma smiled. "I'm ready," she said. She opened the buttons of her trenchcoat. Bobbin looked over, gulped, and reached to button them back up.

"Hey, this is Middle America," he said. "Hold that."

"Okay," she said. "Reverend Muckley, you say?"

"Yes."

"I'll be very nice to him. Very, very nice." ,

"No, no," Bobbin said. "That's just what I don't want."

"What don't you want?" Flamma asked.

"I don't want you giving him any," Bobbin said. "Keep him sniffing around you to keep him interested. But don't give him any."

He seemed very sure of himself and Flamma said "I understand," but she didn't understand at all. Everything she had ever gotten in life, she had gotten by giving some away. Maybe twenty years ago, you kept a man interested by not giving him any, but now you kept a man interested by giving him some right away and making sure it was good. Because if not you, someone else.

But she decided to trust Will Bobbin. She had to. He was her only chance into the movies right now.

Bobbin ushered her into Reverend Muckley's office past the secretary who glared at them coolly, as if sensing that underneath the tan trenchcoat was a threat to her own 38-22-36 supremacy.

Muckley gulped when Flamma stood in front of his desk, smiling at him. He insisted that Bobbin wait outside because he wanted to verify for himself the accuracy of the woman's story.

Bobbin waited on a soft chair in the outer office. He heard the sound of footfalls inside Muckley's office. He heard furniture being moved. So did the secretary. She went to Muckley's office door and turned the knob. The door was locked. She swore to herself and went back to her desk without looking at Bobbin.

A few moments later, the door was unlocked and opened a crack. Flamma winked at Bobbin. "Okay," she called. "I'm doing what you said." She ran from the door, slamming it behind her. Bobbin heard the sound of Reverend Muckley whooping.

After another five minutes, Flamma opened the door and gestured Bobbin to come inside. Muckley was behind his desk, panting heavily. Disappointment shrouded his face. As Bobbin came in, Flamma whispered, "It's all right. But it was close."

"I have checked this young lady's story," Muckley panted, "to my own satisfaction."

"And?"

"And I think it is just what we need to show the people of this area what a sex-drenched beast like Weston Price has in mind for them. I will call the television people here this afternoon."

"All right," Bobbin said. "And Flamma, I'm out of it, remember?"

She nodded. "I know. I read that the Reverend Muckley was here and I volunteered to help him in his battle against the antichrist because I saw the light and realized that what Wesley was planning to do was evil."

Bobbin nodded. "You might tell the television men that Pruiss was going to make a dirty movie with you in it, but that you didn't want stardom that way. You'd pass up stardom if it had to come that way."

"For stardom, I'd eat dogshit in the street," Flamma said.

"I know that and you know that," Bobbin said. "But trust me. Do it my way. It'll make you more mysteri-

124

ous and the movie offers will come pouring in. You'll see."

"Keen," she said.

"And leave me out of it," Bobbin said.

"Cool," said Flamma.

"Of course," said Reverend Muckley.

CHAPTER NINE

"Chiun, I'm confused," Remo said.

"Birds fly and fish swim," Chiun said.

"Meaning?"

"Why are you always surprised when things follow their natural order?" Chiun said. "Who is a better person to be confused than you?"

"If you're going to be snotty, I'll take my problem somewhere else."

"Proceed," said Chiun majestically.

"I don't have any lead on this assassin. Theodosia says oil people but I don't know. I've got Smith checking out Rachmed, who's a sleazy creep. And there's that illiterate minister in town. I don't know."

"It is not unusual," Chiun said.

"Dammit, Chiun, this is important. Will you stop trying to score points off me?"

"All right. I apologize."

"Apologize?" said Remo. "You actually said apologize?"

"Yes."

"That's the first time you ever apologized for anything," Remo said.

He sat back on the bed in his room, staring in wonderment at Chiun who stood against in front of the open window, practicing his shallow breathing exercises.

"Perhaps I never had a reason before to apologize," Chiun said.

"In more than ten years, you think this is the first time you've owed me an apology?"

"Yes," Chiun said. "But I didn't realize you were going to be so ungracious about it. Consider it withdrawn."

"Too late," Remo said. "I already accepted it."

Chiun shrugged and kept looking out the window. Remo shook his head. Something was wrong. Chiun would fight for hours, normally before giving up on a major point like an apology. Something was on his mind.

"Chiun, what do you know about this assassin? What about the silver knife with the horse on it? What aren't you telling me?"

Chiun sighed. "Wait," he said, and went to one of his trunks and carefully removed a white robe from it. He went into the bathroom to change out of his blue morning robe.

Remo recognized the brocaded white robe as Chiun's teaching garment. He put it on when he was going to tell Remo something of great importance. All too often, the thing of great importance turned out to be a lecture on the beauties of Ung poetry or the proper way to steam a fish or how to chew rice into a liquid and extract all its nutrition, without swallowing any of its solid pulp.

Chiun came back and slowly sank into a sitting

position on the floor facing Remo. He settled as softly as dust particles landing on furniture in an unused room.

He folded his hands inside the sleeves of his white kimono and looked dolefully at Remo, who resisted the impulse to tell Chiun to get on with it. With an American, he would do that. With Chiun, all things came in due time, due time often being long after Remo's attention span had been stretched to its limits, then shattered.

"This is very important," Chiun said, "so you will kindly pay attention."

"Yes, Little Father."

"You know that in the past I have occasionally spoken less than highly of certain Oriental peoples," Chiun offered.

"Occasionally?" Remo said. "If I remember it right, the Chinese are slothful and eat cat meat, the Japanese are grasping and avaricious and the Vietnamese would insert it into a duck if the opening was bigger."

"Please," Chiun said. "Whose story is this?"

"Yours, Little Father. Go on," Remo said.

"It is true the Japanese are grasping and avaricious, and that is why I always tell you to have no dealings with them because one never knows when they will turn on you."

"Right. Got it," Remo said impatienly.

"I had not wanted to tell you this until you were older," Chiun said.

"Chiun, I'm a grown man."

"In the ways of Sinanju, but a child. With much to learn."

"Right. Much to learn."

Remo looked ceilingward. He wondered who had

put up the ceiling tile. He could see blue-point nails in the cracks between the crumbly cardboard tiles.

"The Japanese are also given to much exaggeration. For instance, they pretend that their emperors were descended from the sun goddess."

"Right. Sun goddess," Remo said. He wondered about the golf course Pruiss had closed down when he took over the clubhouse. Did it play long or short? Where there many water holes? He'd have to go out and walk it sometime.

"This belief of the Japanese is untrue as are most of their beliefs." Chiun paused. "Remo. I don't really know how to tell you this."

"Right. Don't know how to tell me." Maybe he'd play a round of golf before he left.

"There was a tribe in Korea once called the Koguryo," Chiun said. "They were a fierce and warlike people from the south who overran much of what is now northern Korea. That, of course, is where the village of Sinanju is."

"Right," Remo said. "Sinanju in the north." He stopped and thought a moment. "These kukuru . . ." he said.

"Koguryo," Chiun corrected.

"Did they conquer Sinanju?" Remo asked.

"Of course not," Chiun said. "It is written in the annals of Sinanju that they attempted to do that but the Master of Sinanju—this was not the great Wang because it was before his time—mobilized the people of the village and drove them off. In fact. so great were their losses that the Koguryo left North Korea and returned to the southern part of that country."

"So?"

"So their warlike ways had impressed many of the Sinanju village. And many of the youth chose to ride away with them. Among them were the men of a family called Wa."

"I see," said Remo who was beginning to fade again. What did any of this have to do with the assassin? Koguryo? Wa? Who cared?

"Now you may not understand this, Remo," said Chiun, "because all you white people have big heads and big noses and big feet and big hands. But in a land like Korea where people are the correct size, they look different upon such things as size. The people of this Wa family were very small. In fact, Wa means 'little people.' Often, the children of the village made fun of the Wa family because they were tiny. For this reason, they went to the Master of Sinanju and they said, 'Glorious Master, the people mock us because of our small size. What is it that we may do about this because it is unfair.'"

Chiun paused again.

"And the Master—did I tell you this was not the great Wang?"

"Right. Not the great Wang," Remo said.

"Good. The Master then said, "'A man's courage or skill is not shown by the size of the body surrounding his heart. The people are wrong. And you must learn to win the villagers' admiration for your acts.' He told them they must become expert at some thing and this would make the people admire them and stop their insults.

"'What kind of thing?' he was asked, because the Wa were a very stupid family, as is often the way with people who are too small," Chiun said.

"And the Master said 'Learn to use a weapon with great skill. They will admire your skill and then will not make fun of your size. And even those who are too foolish to admire skill will fear the result of yours and so they will no longer mock you either. This way will you prevail.'"

"Right," Remo said. "Prevail."

"So, with the help of the Master, the Wa practiced and through generations they became experts with knives and people no longer laughed at them because of their small size. But, given respectability, they now yearned for power. So when the Koguryo attacked Sinanju, instead of using their skills to help the village, they made a secret agreement with the invaders that they would assassinate the Master and this would leave the village defenseless."

Remo straightened his back and began to listen. He had heard the word knives in there somewhere. Besides Chiun's voice had risen in intensity and pitch, which meant he was about to tell of people trying to commit the most terrible crime of all, trying to zap the Master of Sinanju.

Chiun looked at Remo as if for confirmation that this was a terrible act by the Wa people. Remo tried to look saddened.

"But, of course they failed," Chiun said. "Even though the skill of their blades had been given them by the Master himself, the pupils were no match for the teacher and he turned away their blades when they fell upon him and he did away with the Wa family. Except for one. This one, the third eldest son, fled. The Master took one of the knives from one of the bodies that surrounded him and on the blade, with his fingernail, he etched the outline of a horse because this was the symbol of an outsider in those days and he tossed the knife after the son who fled. And he told him that forever after he would be an outcast from the Village of Sinanju and that he should go with his Koguryo Masters and do their bidding and many such insults did he visit upon the unfortunate Wa." Chiun smiled as he imagined that ancient Master winning the word battle with the third eldest Wa, while bodies were stacked knee deep around him.

"Those Wa were always sneaky," Remo said, hoping the comment was appropriate.

"Correct," said Chiun. "I am pleased that you are listening. The Master also leveled a curse upon the House of the Wa in a special poem he made up for the occasion."

"Please, Chiun," Remo said, "no poems."

"It is a very important poem," said Chiun.

"Let's keep moving right along," Remo said.

"It is a very short poem," Chiun said.

"It can't be short enough," said Remo. "What happened to the remaining Wa?"

Chiun looked hurt.

"The Wa survivor went away with the Koguryo and they returned to the southern part of Korea to Kaya Province from which they emanated. Soon they controlled all of the South but the appetite of the conqueror is never sated and because they knew the Master awaited them if they again went north, instead they went east, across the Sushima Strait and into Japan's Kyushu Island. They built boats to carry their horses because there were no horses in Japan at that time. By now, the crafty Wa had become the chief advisor to the leader of the Koguryo."

Chiun stopped as if that was the end of the story.

"Well?" asked Remo.

"That is it," said Chiun. "Except for the poem."

"No, no. That can't be it," Remo said. "I know there must be more than that."

"If you insist upon my filling in every little blank spot. . . ."

"I do," Remo said.

"The Koguryo quickly conquered all of Japan because the people who were there then had no ability at all to defend themselves and the Koguryo were warlike and fearsome and besides they had the Wa to advise them and that is that."

"A few questions," Remo said.

"Why must you always ask questions when a story is perfectly clear?"

"You're telling me that this Kukuru . . ."

"Koguryo," Chiun said.

"They conquered Japan?"

"Correct."

"How long did they stay there?" Remo asked.

"Very long."

"What happened to the real Japanese?" Remo asked.

"They were eliminated by the order of the Wa," Chiun said. "All died. All but a few who hid in the north of Japan and still hide there today. These are called the Ainu, and they are a large, white-haired, hairy people."

"So what you're telling me is that the Japanese emperors aren't descended from the sun goddess or whatever but from these Korean horseback riders."

Chiun nodded sadly.

"You mean that the Japanese that you're always abusing are really Koreans who came across on boats?"

"You might say that if you were unkind," Chiun said. His hazel eyes blazed.

Remo laughed. "You mean you're related to Japanese?"

Chiun turned his head away angrily.

134

"What happened to the Wa?" Remo asked.

"He became the counselor, protector and bodyguard of king and emperor alike. He had many children who followed in his footsteps and to them he taught the ways of the knife as the Master, who was not the Great Wang, had taught them so many years before."

"And you think the guy who knifed Pruiss is one of the Wa?" Remo asked.

Chiun nodded. "I had heard their services were on the market. In the building across the street, I saw where the assassin stood. It was a spot where your weight made the floorboards creak. But they did not creak under my weight. The assassin was no heavier than me. And below there were other clues. The distance he had chosen for his attack. The angle of the knife wound. Then we saw on the grass below how he dragged the bodies of men across the grass because he had not the physical strength to carry them. He is a Wa, and this makes it very dangerous."

"For who?" Remo asked.

"For you," said Chiun.

"Why for me?"

"You would not hear the poem. It answers all," Chiun said.

"All right, all right. The poem," Remo said.

Chiun nodded again, as if the recitation were his right. "You will remember, I told you the Master visited a curse upon the surviving Wa. That is the poem."

"What is it?" asked Remo.

"The Master said . . . it does not translate very well."

"Just give me the outlines," Remo said.

"The Master said to the Last Wa:

Because I have trained you in this evil,
I must be punished for your misdeeds.
I punish myself by not allowing myself
to come after you and kill you.
This is my penance.
But, hear you this, evil one.
Through the countless ages of time
will my sons hunt your sons.
I give this duty to generations unborn.
Young Masters of Sinanju will search out
the Wa and kill them whenever they find them.
That is my curse. And your destiny.

This did the Master tell the Wa."

Chiun looked at Remo. "You understand now why this is dangerous for you?"

"No," Remo said.

"You are really a lump of clay," Chiun said. "I am the reigning Master of Sinanju. The Master's curse prevents me from striking down the Wa. You alone must do it, without my help."

Remo shrugged. "So we're facing a Sinanju-trained assassin," he said.

"Yes," said Chiun. He hung his head in shame.

"And the Japanese that you're always putting down are really your relatives," Remo said.

Chiun said nothing.

"You ought to be ashamed of yourself," Remo said.

Chiun looked up. "Remember," he said, "the Wa Japanese are not descended from the villagers of Sinanju. Just from the Koguryo who were an ugly people, whose only skill was in riding a horse."

"I never want to hear you putting down the Japanese again," Remo said. He shrugged. "Anyway, none of this helps. We still don't know who the Wa is working for. Who hired him?"

Chiun smiled. "Who knows? The Japs are a greedy and avaricious people. They'd work for anybody."

He rose swiftly to his feet indicating the lesson was over.

The telephone in the room rang and Smith's parched voice said, "You should know that Will Bobbin is in town."

"Who?"

"Will Bobbin," said Smith. "He flew in last night. He represents the fossil fuel industry, right out of their main New York offices."

"All right. I'll watch for him."

"And the passenger list showed that a woman who traveled only as Flamma arrived in Furlong County this morning."

"Got it," said Remo. He was still thinking about Will Bobbin's arrival. Perhaps Theodosia was right and the oil companies were behind the attack on Pruiss. Perhaps they had hired the Wa assassin to do him in.

"And we have the rundown on Rachmed Baya Bam that you asked for," Smith said.

"What's he all about?"

"He heads something called the Inner Light church. As far as we can make out, he is the only member, but he seems to make a living by being adopted by the rich. His brother is an Indian delegate to the United Nations."

"Baya Bam," Remo said. "The one who's always making anti-American speeches?"

"Yes," said Smith. "That one. From what we can gather, Rachmed is a pickpocket and was arrested once in Yankee Stadium at a World Series game. His brother's diplomatic immunity got him freed. And there are stories that the two of them run a particularly odious brothel in India, specializing in young girls."

After Smith had hung up, Remo went to Theodosia's apartment at the end of the broad hallway. She was sitting in a satin robe, facing a dressing table, putting fresh makeup around her eyes. Remo walked in without knocking and she looked up at him in surprise that softened to a smile of welcome. He saw his motel room keys on the dressing table.

Remo stood behind her, put his right hand on her shoulder and inspected her face in the mirror. He still found it hard to believe. Twenty-two steps and she had been almost impervious to them. That had never happened before. Chiun had once told him that Korean women were regularly exposed to all twenty-seven steps of "the method" as he called it, but Remo had seen the Korean women of Chiun's ancient village of Sinanju and he suspected that the twenty-seven steps might have been as much for the man's benefit as the woman's—to give him something to think about besides his partner and what she looked like.

"Do you know a woman named Flamma?" Remo asked.

"Flamma? What do you know about her?" Theodosia said. She turned on her bench to look at Remo.

"Who is she?" Remo asked.

"She works sometimes for Wesley," the young woman said. "She . . . er, entertains for him."

"What kind of work is . . . er, entertains?" Remo asked.

Theodosia paused. "Okay," she said, as if forcing herself to tell the truth. "She's kind of on the payroll

138

CHAPTER TEN

The Reverend Higbe Muckley had not gotten where he was by being insensitive to how television worked.

Morning press conferences were no good. First, reporters liked to sleep late. Second, from a morning press conference, they would be reassigned to an afternoon story too, and they would get to thinking they were overworked, so they were grouchy, bad audiences in the morning.

Afternoon press conferences usually got cut short because TV men had to get their film back to the studio and hustle to write their story in time for it to get on the six o-clock evening news. If their piece was late, they might get squeezed out of the program by some story that was filmed earlier.

Muckley had learned this by watching television and figuring. The optimum time for a press conference was noon, give or take a half-hour, based on the following indisputable rules:

1. A reporter had a chance to get up and sober up.

2. It gave him a free lunch and he could still bill his station for a lunch cost.

3. It gave him plenty of time to complete and file his story.

4. If the invitation came from a sexy-voiced woman, the lure was irresistible.

So Muckley got his secretary, Sister Corinne, on the telephone right away, alerting the television people that he would hold a press conference at noon and he had proof of "a conspiratorial plot by Wesley Pruiss, a plot so cruel and evil that it would stagger their minds." The secretary read this from a card that Muckley had printed out for her. Then, also at Muckley's directions, she dropped a hint that a former employee of Pruiss's, a one-time Grossie Girl, would be at the press conference. And there would be plenty to eat and drink.

While she was making the calls, the secretary glanced frequently at the office door, worried because she had heard it being locked to keep her out. What were they doing in there?

Inside the office, Muckley and Flamma were discussing the costume she would wear to the press conference. She had a model's hatbox with costumes in it.

"How about this one?" she asked, holding up two flimsy pieces of nylon.

"I don't know," Muckley said. "Better try it on."

"Where can I change?" she said.

"You can change here," he siad. "I'll turn my back."

He turned away from Flamma and watched her in the window as she peeled off her raincoat and put on the costume. She smiled at his reflection as she dressed.

"Done," she said.

Muckley turned and gulped. The nylon costume

142

was transparent, her breasts totally visible. The rest of the outfit was a pair of brief panties covered over with thin nylon pantaloons that showed every pore, every rippling smooth muscle of her long legs.

"What do you think?" Flamma asked.

Muckley came close to inspect her. He walked around her as she stood in the middle of the room. He gulped several times as he eyed her milky body.

"I don't think there's anything wrong with the human body, you understand," he said. "Under the proper circumstances, I think it is the most beautiful of God's creations." He cleared his throat. "And, of course, your body is exceptional. From a purely esthetic viewpoint, that is."

"Of course," said Flamma. She had heard that many times before.

"But I'm afraid, for television, this won't quite work. With lights, it might turn out a little too transparent and then they might not be able to use their film. What else you got in there?"

She reached in and brought out a red satin bra.

"How's this?"

"That might do. Try it on."

"Okay," she said, purposely forgetting to tell him to turn his back again. She reached behind her for the bra clip of the transparent top but pretended she couldn't reach it.

"Can you help me?" she asked.

"Of course, girl," he said. He fumbled with the clip. The palms of his hands were wet with perspiration.

"How long have you been a dancer?" he asked.

"Well," Flamma said, "I'm not really much of a dancer. I can do a turn or two, I guess. But really what I'm good at is tricks. Straight, half-and-half, around the world."

Muckley gulped as the bra clip opened. He let his fingers linger on the bare flesh of her back.

"Of course, you're not going to say that at the press conference," he said.

"Why not?"

"We don't want to harm your credibility. You and me, we're people of the world. We'd understand how some forces could push a young woman into such a life."

Flamma shook her head as she removed her bra. "Nothing forced me. I like it. I always liked it. I still like it. I'd rather do it than anything."

"I can understand that," Muckley said solemnly. "After all, people have needs, desires." He tried to chuckle but it came out like a chicken squawking as its neck was being wrung. "Even us men of the cloth have needs," he said, "although most people would try to deny us. They don't understand the heavy burden we bear, trying to be an example for other people and still having to live with the fires that rage within us." His hands were still on her back.

"You got fires raging in you?" she asked.

"All the time. But I suppress them," Muckley said. He slid his hands toward both sides of her back. Only eight inches more each and he would have those beautiful breasts in his hands.

She leaned forward suddenly, pulling away, lowering her breasts into the red satin top. "You shouldn't suppress them," she said casually. "It'll give you pimples."

She straightened up, her hands behind her on the two bra straps. "Clip that, Rev, will you?"

He clipped the bra closed.

She stepped away from him and turned around, her breasts jutting toward him, two mounds of pleasure

144

and beauty. He had not thought of his bible in a long time, but the Song of Solomon forced its way into his head. Something about breasts.

"How's that?" she said.

"Beautiful," he said, staring at her bosom. "Excruciatingly beautiful."

"Me or it?" she asked. She put her hands under her breasts and lifted them, arranging them inside the bra top.

"You forget, I'm just a man," he said.

"There," she said as she finished adjusting herself. "Now what do you think?"

He looked at her bosom through the red satin. "Just a moment," he said. "There's a wrinkle there." He reached forward and touched the underside of her right breast with his fingers as he adjusted the thin piece of satin.

He let his fingers stay there.

"Okay now?" she asked.

"Fine," he said, still not moving his fingers.

"All right," she said. "I'll slip on the bottoms and then I'll get some breakfast before the press conference."

Muckley looked glum.

"And then," she said.

"And then?" he asked.

She leaned forward and whispered in his ear. He let his hands slide down her back to the round mounds of her buttocks. He kneaded them as Flamma told him in detail, full, glorious colorful detail exactly what she had in mind for the two of them after the press conference was over.

"Praise God," said Rev. Higbe Muckley.

The reporters were bored when Muckley appeared.

They had been assigned to the Pruiss story for two days, most of them, and with the exception of the small picketing at the country club, which ended before they got there, there had been nothing. No groundswell of opinion in the farm country against the porn publisher; no sense of impending violence, no bomb threats, no death threats, no sign of the person or persons who had put the knife in Pruiss's back.

They were prepared to let Muckley die on his feet so they could get to the booze. Furlong County was the dullest place in the world anyway.

But they came to attention when Flamma arrived, stepping out on the small stage next to Muckley and wearing her belly dancer costume. She told them that Pruiss had planned to make Furlong County into the porn movie capital of the world. She told them that she had been going to star in his first movie, but that the Reverend Muckley had saved her by giving her religion.

They wanted to know about that first motion picture.

"It's called *Animal Instincts*," she said.

"What's it about?"

"About a man and his wife who find happiness in nature. She has her collie. He has her, a goat, three girlfriends and me. I'm the lead, because I bring them together again. All at once."

"Goats and dogs?" one reporter asked.

"Yes," she said haltingly. She covered her face with her hands as if crying. "There is no limit to the degradation of Wesley Pruiss and the perverts who are close to him and how he gets people to do his dirty work for him. Thank heavens I have been spared."

Some reporters tried to get her to dance for them, but Flamma demurely said no. Near the end of the press meeting, one reporter asked her for her future plans. They don't include anything with you, Flamma thought, when she found out that the man represented a small Indiana paper.

She took a deep breath, which never failed to draw the reporters' attention. "I plan to pick up the pieces of my life," she said slowly. "Perhaps go back to dancing school. Unless, of course, something else comes up. I think I can entertain people and bring them happiness in a good clean way and that is God's work too." She winked at the reporter for the *National Star*. A two-page color spread in the *Star* and she'd be on her way.

Higbe Muckley finished the press conference by announcing it was now a fight between God-fearing good people and the forces of evil represented by Wesley Pruiss. He ranted and raved some and was going to announce a full schedule of meetings and protests but cut it short when he saw Flamma talking to the reporter from the *Star*, who got up from his seat and headed toward the door with her.

"We march on Pruiss this afternoon," Muckley yelled and jumped from the platform to follow Flamma before anybody else got his hooks into her.

The local television stations rushed the interview onto the tube and Theodosia saw it with Remo and Chiun inside Pruiss's room. He was awake and he growled when he saw Flamma telling of his iniquities.

"That bitch," he said.

"She always was," Theodosia said. "And now those oil people have their hooks in her, she's liable to say or do anything."

"If you see her, you tell her," said Pruiss, "that she's

through. I'm getting somebody else to pose with the Mako shark."

"Good," said Chiun. "The best revenge is living well."

"Try that when you're a cripple," Pruiss said.

"You live well," Chiun said, "by doing those things you are able to do. You can still print things. You can print great work. You can bring beautiful art to thousands of people. Have you ever heard Ung poetry?"

"I don't like much poetry," Pruiss said.

"You will like this," Chiun promised. He began to talk in Korean, a clacking series of throbs and gutturals that only occasionally rhymed.

Pruiss looked in desperation at Remo who shrugged. Chiun was gently waving his hands in front of his body now, one hand opening and closing, the other fluttering back and forth.

"This is the good part," Remo said. "A report on weather conditions in Korea, day by day, for two centuries."

Chiun kept chattering. There was a swelling noise from downstairs and Remo went to the window to watch. The Reverend Muckley was back, but this time leading a mob of more than two hundred people, chanting and carrying signs.

"What's that?" Pruiss said nervously. "What's that?"

Theodosia stood alongside Remo at the window, looking down as the crowd swerved off the main road and advanced on the country club. There were a dozen newsmen and TV cameramen with them.

"What is it?" Pruiss shouted.

"Pickets," Theodosia said. "I'm going to call our police to make sure they don't cause any trouble."

"Are you listening to this?" Chiun asked Pruiss.

148

Chiun turned to Remo. "Will you please see that they keep things quiet down there?" he asked.

"Yes, Little Father," Remo said.

Higbe Muckley took up a position in front of the main door. The crowd swelled around him. He waited until the cameramen had positioned themselves on the steps of the house and then he raised a bullhorn at his side and invoked God's blessing on Wesley Pruiss.

"Damn you, evil one," he called. "Damn you. Are you listening, evil one?"

The house was silent.

"Are you listening?" Muckley shouted into the amplifier.

Chiun went to the window and called out, "He's trying to listen to me. Will you be quiet, fat person?" He turned to Remo. "Remo, will you take care of them, please, before I have to go do it myself." Chiun went back and sat alongside Pruiss's bed and said, "I'll start over, so you don't miss any of it."

Pruiss's eyes flashed from side to side, the eyes of a trapped animal. They grew even more desperate as Remo walked toward the door of the room.

Downstairs, Muckley shouted into the bullhorn. "We know, Pruiss. Thanks to one good woman, we know your evil plan to ruin our community. Do you hear that, evil one? We know.

"We know something else, Pruiss. We know that sometimes we have to be God's instruments ourselves, and we're going to do it, Pruiss. You're not turning this town into a cesspool like the kind you're used to, Pruiss."

Remo slipped out the back door of the building and came around to stand in the crowd.

"We're going to stop you, Pruiss," Muckley bel-

149

lowed. His amplified voice echoed off the house and rebounded out over the valley of the golf course. "Whatever it takes to stop you, evil one, we're going to stop you. The right will triumph."

From inside the house, Remo could hear Chiun's anguished cry, and he knew that if he didn't want the country club surrounded by two hundred dead bodies, he had better move.

Remo selected the best looking housewife he could find in the crowd, stroked her left buttock and before she could turn moved into another spot in the crowd. She looked around wildly. "Hey, she said. "Who did that? Stop that." She glared at the man behind her, a man who looked as if he would take offense at someone squeezing toilet tissue. "Why'd you do that?" she demanded.

"I didn't . . ." the man started.

Muckley turned and glared at the crowd, waiting for silence. Remo lifted a man's wallet from his back pocket. He did it too smoothly and the man did not feel it so Remo clumsily jammed his hand into the man's hip pocket and rummaged around for a while until the man's attention went to his wallet. Remo dropped the billfold on the ground and moved into the crowd.

The man turned around and looked at the man behind him. "Thief," he yelled. "Damned pickpocket thief."

"What?" said the second man, a burly man with a crew cut and a green plaid shirt.

"You heard me. Keep your dirty hands out of my pockets."

The woman was still shouting, working herself up. "You heard me, you pervert," she yelled at the delicate looking man behind her who tried to shrink away.

Muckley tried shouting over the noise. "We are sending you back to the Sodom and Gomorrah you came from, Pruiss," he intoned.

A scuffle started in the crowd. Remo helped it along by goosing two women and jabbing elbows into the ribs of two men, then disappearing from between them.

The first woman slapped the man behind her. The two men were on the ground battling over the wallet. A flurry of fistfights broke out. Wesley Pruiss was forgotten. So was Higbe Muckley. The cameramen came off the porch and toward the crowd to film the fights. Remo reached from behind one man, grabbed one of the TV cameras, and threw it to the ground.

"Press brutality," the cameraman shouted. "Reactionary," he yelled. The man he was yelling at threw a punch.

"Fascist," screamed the other reporters as they retreated back to the relative safety of the porch.

Remo moved away out of the crowd and back upstairs through a rear door of the building.

Chiun glared at him when he came into Pruiss's room.

"Remo, really," he said. "I ask you to keep it quiet. This is how you do it?" He gestured toward the window, through which could be heard the sounds of the police arriving and wading into the mob, breaking up the fights.

"Now I'll have to start all over again," he said.

Pruiss looked at Remo as if inviting pity.

Remo nodded to him. "Pruiss, you've never been safer than you are now."

"Why?" Pruiss asked.

"Chiun never lets an audience get killed."

Remo met Theodosia in the hall.

"Good work," she said.

"Not done yet," Remo said.

"What else?"

"I'm going to go talk to that Muckley. I want to find out if someone put him up to coming here."

CHAPTER ELEVEN

Eight persons were arrested after the brawl in front of the country club but Rev Higbe Muckley was not one of them, and a half hour later, he found himself sitting on the edge of the Wanamaker River. He needed to be alone to think. He had a serious problem.

Where was Flamma?

When she had left the press conference with that reporter from the *Star*, they had told somebody they were on their way to Pruiss's house. But it hadn't fooled Muckley. He knew they were going to a motel right away. His belly tingled at the thought of Flamma in her red satin costume. He had tried calling the reporter's room, but there was no answer.

Where were they?

If that reporter was putting it to her, Muckley'd fix him. He'd fix them both.

He sat on the edge of the river, idly tossing pebbles out into its slow-moving waters. He let his mind drift to the demonstration at the country club. It had gotten untidy and ragged at the edges but it didn't matter. It would be on the news tonight, along with the charges he and Flamma had made at the press conference, and tomorrow when they marched again, their numbers would be larger, and inside of three days, half the people of Furlong County would be marching behind Higbe Muckley. And that would be that for Wesley Pruiss. There would be no alternative but for him to leave Furlong County.

Muckley did not doubt for a moment that the public would now support his crusade. Pruiss had almost weaseled his way into success by promising to cut taxes in the county. But he had forgotten that sex outplays money all the time. Odd that Pruiss of all people should have forgotten that, since sex was the cornerstone of his own empire.

Muckley began to think about the anti-sex sentiment in the country. There might be a way to tap into it. National crusades against smut. Collect money and use some of it to finance legal complaints by some association against smut peddlers, the rest of course to go for administrative costs, which meant Higbe Muckley. Not an association. A church. It would have to be a church for all the tax benefits.

Forgotten now was Flamma as Muckley began to zero his thoughts in on his first love—cash.

A new name for a new church. The Divine Right church was okay for what it did but it didn't have the sock that anti-pornography would need.

The Clean Living church. The Church for Clean Living. He idly fingered a few more pebbles and tossed them into the river. Killyfish first bolted from the splash of each stone, then darted back in after it, searching for food.

A hundred thousand members at ten dollars a head

each year. A million gross. He could get all the work done for less than a quarter of that. The rest to go to Higbe Muckley.

He wished that he had learned to read and write when he was a child. He was okay doing numbers, but if he had been able to write, he could have saved all those legal fees for the Church of Clean Living. He could write the anti-porn briefs himself.

He tossed more pebbles into the stream and wondered if there was a way to increase the net of the Church of Clean Living from seventy-five percent of the gross to something higher. Maybe he could hire cheaper lawyers.

The secretary in Muckley's office had seemed glad to tell him where he could find the preacher. She seemed angry at Muckley, almost hoping that Remo could bring some kind of irritation to his day. She took a deep breath and gave Remo her address too, so he could come around that night and tell her all about his meeting with Higbe Muckley.

Remo promised to and then he was out in the woods leading toward the Wanamaker River, moving silently, not because he tried to, but because it was the only way he knew how to move. Years of training, running along wet strips of soft tissue, spinning, leaping and jumping on the paper with the goal being not to tear it or even wrinkle it had made the soft, slow movement of the langorous cat the only way he moved now.

Someone else was moving toward Higbe Muckley, but Muckley heard nothing except the kerplunking of the small stones he tossed into the river. If Flamma had belly-danced up behind him now, finger-rings clicking and a balalaika plinking away, he might not have heard, because he was concentrating only on money.

So he did not hear the step behind him. He did not hear the whir as a knife made one lazy half-turn on its way to meet his back. He felt it only when the blade pierced his spinal column and then there was no longer anything to feel with so he fell face forward, his head between his feet, arms extended in front of him, like a man doing calisthenics and trying to touch his toes.

Remo had heard the whir of the knife. He had stopped. He heard the small sip of a groan from Muckley, and sensing what it was, he growled and ran ahead through the trees.

The assassin heard the growl behind him. He wanted to recover his knife. But his first choice was always to be careful and he sank back into the trees, moving quickly and quietly away from the place he had heard the sound of a man's angry snarl.

Remo saw Muckley at the edge of the river and saw the knife protruding from his back. He did not have to look to see if the man was dead. Remo knew from the location of the wound and the sprawl of the body that Higbe Muckley had taken his last tax deduction.

An anger welled up in him and he wheeled about to face the heavy forest. The blood of his adopted Korean ancestors surged in him and he called out:

"Wa, do you hear my voice?"

The assassin stopped short when he heard his name called, but he did not answer. He listened.

"There is no running from me, Wa," Remo called. "I am going to feed you your own knives."

The assassin wondered who was calling. And how did he know Wa?

"You speak bravely," he called back. Then, to give the other men no chance to fix the sound, he instantly began to move away, parallel to the river.

Remo started slowly toward the spot in the trees where the sound had come from.

"Brave?" he called out. "What do you know of brave, you worthless chip of carrion who kills only those with their backs to you?"

The assassin stopped. For a moment, he considered going back after this insolent white, but he had other things to do. He called out again.

"You will pay for that, white man. You will pay dearly for your insolence. I only regret I cannot extract that payment right now."

Again he moved away from the sound of his own voice.

Remo recognized that the voice had moved from the first time it had sounded and realized what the assassin was doing. There was no point in following him.

"You extract nothing," Remo taunted. "Your people were always cowards and traitors, attacking at night from behind, turning like rats on the only man ever to take pity on them."

The assassin stopped again.

"Pity?" he called. "The Wa need no pity."

"My ancestor, the Master of Sinanju, took pity on you centuries ago," Remo called. "As he did, so I will not. When we meet, Wa, you die."

A chill ran down the assassin's body when he heard "Master of Sinanju." Surely that had been nothing more than a family legend. But why would this . . . this white man know of it?

"Who are you?" he called.

"I am a Master of Sinanju, peanut," Remo called. And he forced his anger inward, until his rage had spent, and then slowly pronounced the words he had spoken so often before.

"I am created Shiva, the Destroyer; death, the shatterer of worlds; the dead night tiger made whole by the Master of Sinanju. Flee, dog meat, for when we meet, there will be no flight for you."

The assassin paused. Remo was not moving. His voice still came from the same spot.

Pride in his art and in his tradition and family almost forced him to return, to cut down this prideful white man with the overactive imagination. A Master of Sinanju indeed? The Wa would teach him of Masters of Sinanju.

"When we meet again," the assassin call, "I will have time for you. It will be my pleasure."

He turned and moved softly away through the woods, and behind him he heard Remo's laugh echoing over the wide river.

And in that prideful laugh, welling out of his throat like the pulsing of the blood in his veins, Remo felt at one and at peace with his ancestors, that generation after generation of assassins who had refined the magic of Sinanju and handed it down through the ages as their legacy to him.

He turned and looked back at Muckley's body.

"That's the biz, sweetheart," he said coldly. "But don't worry. When I meet him, I'm canceling his return ticket."

As soon as Remo entered the room, Chiun knew.

"You have met the Wa," he said.

Remo nodded.

He got away," Remo said. "He left his calling card."

Remo held the red-leather handled knife toward Chiun, just as Theodosia burst into the room.

"I just heard on the television," she said. "Muckley's dead. Knifed."

She saw the knife in Remo's hand and uttered a muffled "oooh."

Her eyes fixed on him, all questions, which Remo did not answer.

Chiun took the knife and looked at the engraved horse on the blade.

"You said you were just going to talk to him," Theodosia told Remo accusingly.

"Easy," he said. "I didn't kill him."

"On television, they're blaming Wesley and his people. That means you. Us. All of us."

"They can blame who they want," Remo said. "He was dead when I got there."

Theodosia nodded, but it was not a convincing statement of agreement.

Before either could speak, the telephone rang and from the first syllable, Remo recognized the annoyed voice of Harold W. Smith.

"I didn't do it," he said.

Remo listened a while, then said, "We'll keep him alive." He hung up, without any pretense of a cordial goodbye.

"Who was that?" Theodosia asked.

"My junior high school gym teacher," Remo said. "He promised to check with me from time to time to see if I was making a success out of my life."

Chiun was carefully examining the knife. Rachmed ran into the room.

"I just heard," he said to Theodosia. "Missss, I do

not mind telling you that I do not like all this killing and violencccccce."

"No," Remo said. "I guess pickpocketing is as violent as you like to get."

Rachmed glared at him. "It was all a mistake, sssir," he said. His face flushed.

"And the whorehouse for little girls? Is that a missssssstake, too?"

Baya Bam ran from the room. Theodosia looked at Remo with suspicion in her eyes. "Just who the hell are you?" she said.

"Your friendly neighborhood bodyguard," Remo said. Chiun put down the knife. Remo said, "Pruiss is all right?"

Chiun nodded toward the wall separating his room from Pruiss's.

"You can hear him breathing, can you not?"

Remo listened and caught the sound of Pruiss's breath. He nodded. Theodosia strained to hear but could hear nothing.

"If it wasn't you, who was it?" she asked Remo. She paused, then answered her own question to her own total satisfaction. "Those oil people. Bobbin," she said. She swore.

She wheeled. Remo and Chiun heard her entering Pruiss's room.

Chiun looked at Remo.

"The game is almost played out, my son," he said. Remo nodded.

"Be careful," Chiun said.

CHAPTER TWELVE

"I didn't know that was going to happen."

Flamma was shoving clothes into a bag. Judging by the size of the red satin garment she was wearing, Remo gauged that the bag—a small model's hat box—would hold enough changes of clothes for an around-the-world trip. Twice. On foot.

"What'd you think was going to happen?" Remo said. He lounged on the bed as Flamma breezed about the small motel room showing him lots of flesh and very little interest.

"I thought they were going to yell at Wesley and embarrass him and that would be that and I'd be even because he wasn't going to make my movie."

"*Sheep Dip*, wasn't it?" Remo asked.

"*Animal Instincts*," Flamma corrected. "But I didn't expect anybody to get killed. Even if the Reverend Muckley *was* an old pervert."

"Who hired you?" asked Remo. He had gotten into her room by showing an old card he carried, one of many, which announced that Remo McElaney was an

161

investigator for the United States Senate Select Sub-committee on Grain Purchases and Natural Resources. He could just as easily have shown her a card listing himself as an FBI agent, a CIA man, a Treasury man, a Jersey City cop, or a field representative for the International Fish and Game Commission. But Grain Purchases and Natural Resources was the first one that had come out of his pocket. Flamma was so nervous she hadn't bothered to look at it closely. People never did.

"Will Bobbin," she answered. "Well, he didn't exactly hire me but he paid my way out here and he promised me a screen test."

"If you run now, you'll blow the screen test," said Remo.

"It's all right. I'm getting two pages in the *National Star*. That'll get me all the screen tests I want," Flamma said. "Anyway, where the hell is Bobbin when I need him? I need protection," she said.

"Why?" asked Remo. "Somebody after you?"

"Who the fuck knows?" she said. Without any seeming regard for Remo's presence, she took off her red satin top and, barebreasted, began to root in a drawer for a thin halter top that she began to put on.

"Who the hell was after Muckley, that twerp?" she asked. "If Wesley's involved, I don't know. That man just may go crazy. He may want us all killed and that dyke with him is just the bitch to do it."

"Theodosia?" asked Remo.

"Right. Theodore," said Flamma.

She had her top on and now she peeled off her red satin G-string. Bottomless and blasé, she rooted around in the drawer for slacks to wear.

She found a pair and began to slip them on.

162

Remo said, "Maybe Bobbin. But why would Bobbin want to have Muckley killed?"

She pulled her trousers up. "Beats me," she said. "Bobbin put me on to Muckley though. I kind of thought they were working together." She shrugged, an ample movement that earthquaked the mountains of her breasts and let them drop. "Some kind of falling out?" she suggested.

"Maybe." Remo got up from the bed. He stood behind Flamma who was tossing her makeup from a dresser drawer into the small bag.

He touched her on the shoulders, then let his fingers move over to one of the long tendons in her neck and began slowly rotating around the skin at the joint of her neck and shoulder.

She lolled her head to one side, like a child being tickled. "Ummmmmm," she said contentedly.

"Where's Will Bobbin now?" Remo asked.

"I don't know. Don't stop that. It feels good. Do all you government men do this?"

"When'd you see him last?" Remo changed his attention to a spot in the center of Flamma's bare back. She arched like a kitten.

"Bobbin? After the press conference," she said.

"Where?"

"A cocktail lounge in town. I was with a reporter and Bobbin was in the bar and he made me promise not to tell the guy who he was. Make bigger circles. I asked him where he was going."

Remo made bigger circles. Flamma reached behind her and pulled Remo's hips closer to her.

"What'd he say?" Remo asked.

"He said he was going to hang around town until Wesley left. He wanted to be sure." She turned and ground her body against Remo.

"You really have to go?" she asked.

"Yeah. Did you forget your plane?"

"I wouldn't mind missing it if you're going to hang around," Flamma said.

"Did you ever see Bobbin with a small Oriental?" Remo asked.

She shook her head and then narrowed her eyes, looking at Remo suspiciously. "What has all this got to do with you?" she asked. "With natural resources?"

"Flamma," said Remo, "you're one of our country's greatest natural resources."

"You're right. Even better than oil, 'cause I don't run dry."

She lifted her mouth to be kissed. Remo pressed his lips against her neck and felt her shudder.

He waited until she was finished packing and put her in a taxicab for the airport. As he watched her drive away, he realized he was no closer to the assassin, and who hired him, than he had been before. But there was a feeling, too, in his stomach that that problem would soon be resolved.

CHAPTER THIRTEEN

Chiun was in Wesley Pruiss's room. Pruiss had his face buried in the pillow as if to stifle some heart-rending personal agony and to prevent the world from seeing his tears. Chiun was reciting the same Ung epic. Remo could tell that, as he came into the room, because Chiun was still making the same hand motions to depict a bee and a flower.

Chiun silenced Remo with an index finger upraised in warning. He had just gotten to the big dramatic part of the epic where the flower opens to greet the morning sun and the bee swoops in.

Remo waited in the doorway but Pruiss saw him and his face grew alive and animated.

"Hey, you," he called. Chiun kept talking. Remo stood as if rooted.

"Come here, will you?" Pruiss said.

Chiun looked at Pruiss, then at Remo, then nodded toward Remo who came forward. As he passed Chiun, the old Korean shook his head sadly: "I think I've lost him somehow."

"You know what they say about casting pearls before swine, Little Father," said Remo.

Chiun went to the window and looked out as Remo stood at Pruiss's bedside. The publisher whispered to him, agonizedly, "Doesn't he ever stop?" He nodded toward Chiun.

"The only way to stop him to is make him mad at you. Tell him you like Chinese poetry better or something. That might work. It's got one drawback though."

"What's that?" Pruiss asked.

"If you make him too mad, he might just fillet you like a flounder. Where's Theodosia?"

"I don't know. I told her to reorder all those solar energy supplies. I heard about Muckley. Was it the same guy who got me?"

Remo nodded. "*And* the three bodyguards," he said.

"The oil companies are bastards," Pruiss said. "I never knew I was getting into this."

"Theo finally convinced you," Remo said.

"Yeah. Well, if they think they're going to frighten me, they got another think coming. I got them by the short hairs," Pruiss said.

"How?"

"I signed some papers a little while ago. If I die, everything goes over to Theodosia. And I told her to tell the press that. That'll let the bastards know we're not going to be scared off. And if that sucker with the knives gets me, then Theo takes over and the energy project goes on anyway. That should make them think twice before coming after me again, right?"

"Dope," Reno said. He shook his head.

"What do you mean?"

"They killed all this many people," Remo said.

166

"What makes you think they're going to worry about just one more? All you've done is add Theo to the target list. Where the hell is she?"

The impact of what he had done finally sank in on Pruiss. His beefy face looked strained and there were tension lines around his mouth. "It was her idea," he sputtered.

"Swell," said Remo in disgust. He wheeled away from Pruiss and went down the hall to look for Theodosia. But her room and Baya Bam's were empty. He searched the woman's room; his motel room key was gone.

"Chiun, I'm going to look for Theo. I think she might be next."

"I will stay here," Chiun said. "This one has not yet heard the ending of my poem."

"Go," Pruiss said in desperation. "Save Theo," he told Chiun.

"A loving heart is the mark of all good men," Chiun said. "But I will stay here nevertheless. You go, Remo. My place is here."

The only vehicle parked downstairs was the Pruiss ambulance and Remo hopped into it and sped from the driveway.

From a vantage point in the trees across from the house, the assassin watched him go. And hoped he would return soon.

Remo pulled the ambulance into the motel parking lot and ran toward the two rooms he and Chiun had shared when they first reached town.

The door to Chiun's room was unlocked and Remo stepped inside. The room was empty.

He turned to leave and then stopped as he heard

167

voices from the adjoining room. He stepped to the connecting door between the rooms.

He heard a telephone being replaced on the receiver.

Then he heard Baya Bam's voice. "Now we can leave," Rachmed said. "And start our new lives together."

"Yeah, sure," come Theodosia's voice in answer. Her voice was surly and bitter.

"What is it, sweet missssss?" asked Baya Bam. "What troubles you?"

"Look, Rachmed," she said, very briskly. "Our business deal is over You were supposed to con Wesley into going ahead with the sun energy project. You did it. That's it. Cold cash. Nothing else."

There was a sinking feeling in Remo's stomach as he listened, and then the feeling seemed to swell back up and turn into a bitter burning anger.

"But our love?" Rachmed said. Remo heard Theodosia laugh. Suddenly everything had become very clear.

"Love?" Theodosia said. "Come off it."

Remo slammed the heel of his hand against the door. It shuddered on its hinges, then swung back into the next room.

"That's right, Rachmed," Remo said as he stepped inside. Theodosia turned to him, her face startled. "She never loved you. You're not her type. No man is. Isn't that right, Theodore?"

Theodosia ran toward him. "Oh, Remo," she said. "I've been so worried." He could almost hear her mind clicking as she thought of what story might work. "We heard the assassin had been seen over here and we . . ."

168

"Nice try," Remo said. He pushed her away, hard, and she fell back onto the bed.

"Ssssir, you are no gentleman," Rachmed hissed.

"Quiet, pimp. You're so dumb you don't even know this bull dyke conned you."

Rachmed looked stupidly confused.

"That's right," said Remo. "Conned. She used you to keep Pruiss involved in the solar energy thing. Then she kept telling him the oil people were after him, and when she got him fired up enough, he signed a paper she gave him that turned everything over to her if anything happens to him. Isn't that right, Theo?"

She looked up at Remo and a hard glint came into her deep brown eyes. She nodded.

"But our love?" Baya Bam pleaded to her.

"Where'd you get him?" Remo asked. "He's got a loose upper-plate."

"He comes cheap," Theodosia said. "You don't. But you don't have any more brains than he's got. When did you catch on?"

"I didn't," Remo said. "When you were cold during sex, I should have gotten a clue about you. But I didn't. It was only today. Flamma said something about the lesbian around Pruiss. She called you 'Theodore.' It didn't register. You know I came here to save you? I still didn't know until I heard you two talking."

The woman glanced at her thin gold wristwatch.

"Waiting for someone?" Remo asked. "Maybe your assassin?"

Theodosia shook her head, a vicious smile spreading her lips wide.

"No," she said slowly. "He's not coming here. Right now, he should be walking into Wesley's house to do

169

the job right this time. No near-misses like I contracted for the first time. In about five minutes, I give or take a couple, Wesley should be dead."

Remo smiled back at her. "Fat chance," he said. "He's got to get past Chiun first. He's got as much chance to swim the Pacific."

"Oh, I forgot to tell you," Theodosia said. "Chiun is on his way here. I just talked to him on the telephone, and told him we had spotted the assassin here. He was worried you might get hurt so he said he'd be right over."

Conned. Even before she spit out the awful cold truth, Remo knew. He had been suckered into leaving Pruiss alone, suckered because he had trusted this woman and feared for her safety.

He turned and ran from the room. There was no time to spend expending his anger. Judgment would have to wait.

Behind him, he heard Theodosia laughing. "Too late," she called. "Too late."

Remo floored the gas pedal of the ambulance as he raced back toward the Pruiss mansion. He realized just how much he was the son of Sinanju now, because he had no feeling for Pruiss, he did not care if the publisher lived or died, but his job was to keep him alive and like Masters of Sinanju for uncounted centuries, he just wanted to do his job.

The puzzle sorted itself out in his mind as he drove. Theodosia had hired the assassin, not to kill Pruiss, but to injure him and frighten him. She had hired the bodyguards just to make it look good and when Remo and Chiun had arrived, she had been forced to hire them too. Rachmed's faith healing was supposed to keep Pruiss interested in solar energy, because Theodosia needed that to justify the story she was ped-

170

dling Pruiss—that the oil interests were after him. And she hammered that story and hammered it and hammered it, until finally she convinced Pruiss and in anger, he turned everything over to her if he should die, with orders to make sure solar energy went through.

If he should die. Right now, that assassin was supposed to be changing "if" to "when."

Only another mile. Almost there.

Chiun had walked from the front door of the house and down the driveway. The assassin had watched him go. The old Oriental had looked both ways, then turned and began to walk rapidly in the direction of the town.

The Wa assassin allowed himself to wonder. Who was this old Oriental? Did he too have some knowledge of Sinanju? What was his relationship with the young, big-mouthed American? As Chiun walked away, the assassin shrugged. His job was to get rid of Wesley Pruiss. But then he would stay around. As a bonus, not for pay but for pleasure, that American would go too. And, if he got in the way, the old Oriental also.

He walked across the practice green toward the front door of the house, where Pruiss now lay, alone. It was not true, the Wa knew. The American had said he struck only from behind, but that was not true. The Wa worked from behind when he had to, for silence, but he would rather work face to face.

He liked to see the faces of his victims, see the shock and horror when they saw him, watch it change to pain and the dumb look of death when the knife struck home. The face and eyes always looked dumb, puzzled, just before death came. That is what he wanted to see now.

He hoped Wesley Pruiss was sitting up in bed so he could see the Wa enter the room. Then the Wa could watch the growing terror as he spoke the words, "I have waited for you," and then the fright and shock as he drew his knife, and Pruiss's desperate crippled efforts to escape, or to plead for his life, and then the whir as the knife flashed across empty space toward the bed and the satisfying thunk as it bit deeply into the throat, crushing Adam's Apple, severing nerves. Then the look of dumb stupidity on the face as death arrived.

And then there would be time for the American who said he was from Sinanju. Sinanju. What was it anyway but a foolish legend?

The Wa moved silently up the stairway of the empty house, his light footfalls making no sound on the thick carpeting. He walked down the center of the hall. His belt of knives was slung low around his hips, in the way Wa assassins had carried their weapons from the time of the very first Wa.

He paused in the center of the hallway. He heard only one sound, that of Wesley Pruiss breathing. It was a soft low sipping of air, the kind of mouth breathing most Americans inflicted on their bodies.

There were no other sounds in the building. He continued walking down the hall, then paused. The door to Wesley Pruiss's room was open.

He reached behind him and took one of the red-handled knives from his leather belt. He held it at his side, then stepped forward, and took two steps into the room.

Wesley Pruiss was propped up on pillows, looking toward the door. His eyes were confused, frightened. The Wa smiled. He extended the knife before him.

He opened his mouth to speak.

And then a voice echoed through the room.

"I have waited for you," said the voice, a strong voice, deep as rolling thunder, and it sent a chill down the spine of the assassin.

He looked toward the right side of the room. Stepping from behind a large wardrobe chest was the aged Oriental, his powder blue robe swirling about him, a thin smile on his parchment face.

He stared at the Wa and the power of those eyes seemed to burn into the assassin's skull. The Wa blinked once, as if to release the bond that connected them, then wheeled toward the aged intruder.

"It is all right, old man," he said. "Now my knives will have two instead of one."

"Fool," intoned Chiun. "I am the Master of Sinanju. My ancestors banished you to far-away lands, and now I banish you to death."

The Wa reached behind him with his left hand to withdraw another knife. Even as he was reaching, his right hand raised up over his head, and the knife flashed across the room toward the open, inviting throat of Wesley Pruiss.

But then, as quick as a spark, the old Oriental flashed across the room. His open fingertips touched the blade of the knife, just a split second before it opened Pruiss's throat, and the knife fell to the floor. The Oriental lay across Pruiss's body, and the Wa saw this was his chance. His left hand came above his head and then down, with all the power in his slim, conditioned body. The knife flew toward Chiun.

It made one slow half-turn and then the point reached the old man's chest. And then, as the Wa watched in horror, the old man's right hand moved down with a speed so blurring it was beyond speed, and he caught the tip of the knife between his fingers,

173

short of its target. He rose to his feet, still holding the spent weapon by its point, and with a smile, extended it toward the assassin. Then he took a step toward the slim young man.

The country club looked quiet and peaceful as Remo rolled the ambulance up to the front of the building. He was out of the vehicle before it finished rocking on its springs. The house looked peaceful but death, he knew, was a peaceful thing. Only amateurs made noise.

As Remo started up the steps of the house, the front door flew open and the Wa assassin raced out. He saw Remo and vaulted the small railing alongside the porch and ran around behind the ambulance to the practice putting green.

Remo looked after him. Chiun appeared at the upstairs window and saw Remo.

"It is all right, Remo," he called. "I saved him for you."

"Thank you, Little Father," Remo said. He walked slowly behind the ambulance to the putting green.

The Wa assassin, his breath coming nervously in short puffs, watched as the American stopped ten feet away from him and waited, hands on hips.

"It's all over, peanut," Remo said.

Not yet, the assassin thought. He had missed upstairs, something that had never happened before. But that was no guarantee that he would miss now. The young white man stood facing him, offering up his body to the assassin's knives, and with both hands at once, the Wa ripped knives from his belt, and flew them toward the waiting victim.

Remo posed, hands on hips, until the knives were almost on him, and then his hands moved. His left hand slashed against the handle of the knife aimed at his throat and knocked it harmless to the ground. His right hand moved only a few inches upward, just barely touching the knife aimed at Remo's eyes, but enough to veer the knife off course. It soared over the white man's head and travelled ten feet more before it buried itself deep into the trunk of a fat tree.

The Wa turned to run. Panic overcame pride in him and he fled. But as he reached the stand of trees, suddenly, there was a movement alongside him, and then the American was standing in front of him, smiling at him.

The Wa turned away. He ran back, across the putting green toward the trees on the other side. But again he saw a flash of movement from the side of his eyes, and then there was the American again.

He was beckoning the Wa to come on, to come closer.

The assassin stopped. In bitter desperation, he cried: "Who are you? Who are you two?"

"Tell your ancestors about us," Remo said. "They'll know who we are."

The Wa reached desperately for one last knife on his belt. One final chance. Even as he reached he knew it would not work, but his hand closed around the red leather grip and he slipped the knife from his belt and raised it up over his head, and then he felt the white man's hand close over his. The Wa's knife moved downward, but the white man held the Wa's hand closed, and the knife, instead of releasing and flashing forward, kept moving down, and then he felt a burst of pressure against his hand, and the knife drove itself into the assassin's stomach.

So this was how it felt, he thought, and then the knowledge that he had a knife buried in his stomach came fully to him, and so did the pain, and it hurt. It hurt terribly.

Remo stepped back and looked at the assassin. Their eyes met.

And then the Wa's eyes began to glaze over and a dumb, puzzled look came over his face, and he fell forward onto his own knife. But he no longer felt any pain.

Remo looked down at the body for a moment, then up at the window of Pruiss's room. Chiun was in the window, shaking his head.

"No grace," he said. "Awkward with no grace."

"That's what I thought, too," Remo said. "I thought he was kind of clumsy."

"I didn't mean him," Chiun said bitterly, and turned from the window.

Remo confronted Chiun inside Pruiss's room.

"All right," he said. "So you get word that the assassin's around and maybe I'm in trouble, and you don't even come to see if you can help me," Remo said. "Fine partner you are."

Chiun folded his arms. "I knew you were in no danger," he said.

"How'd you know, hah? How'd you know?"

"Must we really do this?" Chiun asked.

"Just answer the question. How'd you know I wasn't in any trouble?" Remo demanded.

Chiun sighed.

"When the woman who thinks like a man called, and told me to come to save you, I knew it was a lie," he said.

"How?"

"Because she is not to be trusted. Did you not see

176

when we were at the place of airplanes that she knew a boom . . ."

"Bomb," Remo said.

". . . was going to explode?" Chiun looked at Remo. "No," he answered himself. "You did not see that."

He turned toward the window. "And of course you never asked yourself why the Wa assassin missed the first time. He missed because he was ordered to miss. But who would benefit by keeping this publisher person alive, but damaged? No. You did not ask yourself that either."

"What's going on here?" Pruiss demanded. "What's going on here?" He lay on his pillows watching the two men argue, his head moving from side to side as if watching a tennis match.

"And then of course you told me about your reaching twenty two steps with her and I knew that was not possible for a white woman who acted like a woman. It was obvious she was a manly woman. You would even have seen it if you had looked at the strange size of her masculine fingers. But you look and do not see, look and do not see."

"What the hell is going on here?" Pruiss roared.

"So I knew it was a trick to get me away from here," Chiun said. "And of course I did not go."

"All right," Remo said. "I'll let it go this time."

"What . . ." Pruiss started.

Remo turned to the publisher and told him that Theodosia had been behind it all. Her goal had been to get him to sign his empire over to her, and then to kill him.

Pruiss shook his head.

"What for? Just for the money?"

177

Remo shrugged. "Who knows? Who can figure out lesbians? Probably the money."

"I would have given her the money," Pruiss said. "For that, she left me a cripple?"

"I wanted to speak to you about that," Chiun said. "What would it be worth to you to use your legs again?"

"Anything."

"You will publish my stories?" Chiun asked.

"I'll publish your damn poetry," Pruiss said.

"We have a bargain," Chiun said. "Go to sleep. I must prepare."

He followed Remo out of the room.

"Prepare?" Remo said. "What are you going to prepare?"

Chiun shook his head. "That is just for effect. There is nothing to prepare."

"And you're going to make him walk again?" asked Remo.

"Of course. He can walk now," Chiun said.

"How do you figure that?"

"You did not really believe that that Indian charlatan was bringing life back to his limbs by allowing his legs to sunburn, did you?"

"No. Of course not," said Remo who was not quite that sure.

"But Mister Pruiss felt life in his limbs every morning," said Chiun. "After his sunbath."

"So?"

"And then the manly woman brought him inside again to give him his medicine and he felt no more life in his limbs."

Remo slowly began to nod.

"She called it medicine to kill Mister Pruiss's pain. But I tasted it while you were gone. It is medicine that keeps his limbs paralyzed. I have thrown it away. Without it, tomorrow his legs will return to life."

"You're awful," Chiun," said Remo.

Chiun looked at him with an angelic blank expression.

"Whatever do you mean?" he asked.

"Some people will do anything to get published," he said.

Chiun smiled. "And what of the woman?" he asked.

"I'll take care of her," Remo said. "I'll take care of all of them."

The next morning, when the previous day's medicine had worn off, Wesley Pruiss felt life returning to his legs. The feeling grew stronger all day long.

Two days later, he was able to stand again, and within two weeks he was walking.

A day later he held a press conference and announced that he was returning the ownership of Furlong County to the people of the county who had been "so hospitable and gracious in welcoming me among them." He also announced that he was setting up a private foundation that would go ahead with his plans to make Furlong County the nation's solar energy laboratory, and he would pick up all the bills for the work.

His final announcement was that he was beginning a new magazine. It would be dedicated to bringing to the public a realization of the ancient glories and beauties of the great Korean literary form, Ung poetry.

Pruiss's announcements did not get the kind of Page One coverage they normally would have. Unfortunately, they were crowded off the front pages by a terrible tragedy at the Furlong County Airport.

A gang of muggers, whom no one had seen but who must obviously have been a large gang, had fallen upon three people at the airport—Theodosia, Rachmed Baya Bam and Will Bobbin. In the melee all three were killed. The murder weapons were unusual red-handled knives, with rearing stallions engraved on the blade.

The only person noticed near the scene was a thin, dark-haired white man with thick wrists.

The Number 1 hit man loose in the Mafia jungle . . .
nothing and nobody can stop him from wiping out the
Mob!

the EXECUTIONER
by Don Pendleton

The Executioner *is without question the best-selling action/
adventure series being published today. American readers
have bought more than twenty million copies of the more
than thirty volumes published to date. Readers in England,
France, Germany, Japan, and a dozen other countries have
also become fans of Don Pendleton's peerless hero. Mack
Bolan's relentless one-man war against the Mafia, and Pendleton's unique way of mixing authenticity, the psychology of
the mission, and a bloody good story, crosses all language bar-
riers and social levels. Law enforcement officers, business executives, college students, housewives, anyone searching for a
fast-moving adventure tale, all love Bolan. It isn't just the realism and violence, it certainly isn't blatant sex; it is our guess
that there is a "mystique"—if you will—that captures these
readers, an indefinable something that builds an identification
with the hero and a loyalty to the author. It must be good, it
must be better than the others to have lasted since 1969, when
War Against the Mafia, the first Executioner volume, was
published as the very first book to be printed by a newly born
company called Pinnacle Books. More than just lasting, however—as erstwhile competitors, imitators, and ripoffs died or
disappeared—The Executioner has continued to grow into an
international publishing phenomenon. The following are some
insights into the author and his hero . . . but do dare to read
any one of* The Executioner *stories, for, more than anything
else, Mack Bolan himself will convince you of his pertinence
and popularity.*

The familiar Don Pendleton byline on millions of copies of Mack Bolan's hard-hitting adventures isn't a pen name for a team of writers or some ghostly hack. Pendleton's for real ... and then some.

He had written about thirty books before he wrote the first book in *The Executioner* series. That was the start of what has now become America's hottest action series since the heyday of James Bond. With thirty-four volumes complete published in the series and four more on the drawing board, Don has little time for writing anything but *Executioner* books, answering fan mail, and autographing royalty checks.

Don completes each book in about six weeks. At the same time, he is gathering and directing the research for his next books. In addition to being a helluva storyteller, and military tactics expert, Don can just as easily speak or write about metaphysics and man's relationship to the universe.

A much-decorated veteran of World War II, Don saw action in the North Atlantic U-boat wars, the invasion of North Africa, and the assaults on Iwo Jima and Okinawa. He later led a team of naval scouts who landed in Tokyo preparatory to the Japanese surrender. As if that weren't enough, he went back for more in Korea, too!

Before turning to full-time duty at the typewriter, Don held positions as a railroad telegrapher, air traffic controller, aeronautical systems engineer, and even had a hand in the early ICBM and Moonshot programs.

He's the father of six and now makes his home in a small town in Indiana. He does his writing amidst a unique collection of weapons, photos, and books.

Most days it's just Don, his typewriter, and his dog (a German Shepherd/St. Bernard who hates strangers) sharing long hours with Mack Bolan and his relentless battle against the Mafia.

Despite little notice by literary critics, the Executioner has quietly taken his position as one of the better known, best understood, and most provocative heroes of contemporary literature—primarily through word-of-mouth advertising on the part of pleased readers.

According to Pendleton, "His saga has become identified in the minds of millions of readers as evidence (or, at least, as hope) that life is something more than some silly progression of charades through which we all drift, willy-nilly—but is a meaningful and exhilarating adventure that we all share, and to which every man and woman, regardless of situation, may contribute some meaningful dimension. Bolan is therefore considerably more than 'a light read' or momentary diversion. To the millions who expectantly 'watch' him through adventure after adventure, he has become a symbol of the revolt of institutionalized man. He is a guy *doing something*—responding to the call of his own conscience—making his presence felt in a positive sense—realizing the full potential of his own vast humanity and excellence. We are all Mack Bolan, male and female, young and old, black and white and all the shades between; down in our secret heart of hearts, where we really live, we dig the guy because *we are* the guy!

The extensive research into locale and Mafia operations that make *The Executioner* novels so lifelike and believable is always completed before the actual writing begins.

"I absorb everything I can about a particular locality, and the story sort of flows out of that. Once it starts flowing, the research phase, which may be from a couple of days to a couple of weeks, is over. I don't force the flow. Once it starts, it's all I can do to hang on."

How much of the Bolan philosophy is Don Pendleton's?

"His philosophy *is* my own," the writer insists. "Mack Bolan's struggle is a personification of the struggle of collective mankind from the dawn of time. More than that, even Bolan is a statement of the life principle—*all* life. His killing, and the motives and methods involved, is actually a consecration of the life principle. He is proclaiming, in effect, that life is meaningful, that the world is important, that it does matter what happens here, that universal goals are being shaped on this cosmic cinder called earth. That's a heroic idea. Bolan is championing the idea. That's what a hero is. Can you imagine a guy like Bolan standing calmly on the sidelines, watching without interest while a young woman is mugged and raped? The guy cares. He is reacting to a destructive principle inherent in the human situation; he's fighting it. The whole world is Bolan's family. He cares about it, and he feels that what happens to it is tremendously important. The goons have rushed in waving guns, intent on raping, looting, pillaging, destroying. And he is blowing their damned heads off, period, end of philosophy. I believe that most of *The Executioner* fans recognize and understand this rationale."

With every title in the series constantly in print and no end in sight, it seems obvious that the rapport between Don Pendleton and his legion of readers is better than ever and that the author, like his hero, has no intention of slowing down or of compromising the artistic or philosophical code of integrity that has seen him through so much.

"I don't go along with the arty, snobbish ideas about literature," he says. "I believe that the mark of good writing can be measured realistically only in terms of public response. Hemingway wrote Hemingway because he was Hemingway. Well, Pendleton writes Pendleton. I don't know any other way."

Right on, Don. Stay hard, guy. And keep those *Executioners* coming!

* * *

[Editors note: for a fascinating and incisive look into *The Executioner* and Don Pendleton, read Pinnacle's *The Executioner's War Book*, available wherever paperbacks are sold.]